Confessions of a

Queen B*

The Queen B*, Book 1
by
Crista McHugh

Prologue

In every high school, there are two types of Queen Bs. The first type is the most obvious. With a collection of tiaras and an entourage of drones that follow her wherever she flitters, this Queen Bee practically rules the school (or so she thinks). Get in her good graces, and you're suddenly part of the in-crowd. Wear the wrong brand of skinny jeans, and you'll feel the sting of ostracism.

Me? I'm Alexis Wyndham, and I'm the other type of Queen B.

The Queen Bitch.

Crista McHugh

"Despite the school administration's insistence that they have put an end to the hazing ritual known as Freshman Initiation, these photos demonstrate that it's still alive and well in our hallways. Please note the faculty member in the background watching, but making no move to stop the harassment."

The Eastline Spy
September, Senior Year

Chapter 1

I'd never set out to become the Queen Bitch of Eastline High. After enduring years of being teased and made the butt of practical jokes in middle school, I'd simply decided to start high school three years ago with a new mindset.

I no longer prayed for acceptance or kept my mouth closed.

I was hard.

I was cruel.

I didn't let people get to me.

I was the Queen B.

My fellow students parted like the Red Sea to let me pass when I walked down the hallway. As a senior, I'd either earned most students' respect or their fear. My blog, *The Eastline Spy*, had exposed everything from cheating (both in and out of the classroom) to the subpar food served in the cafeteria. No one wanted to be the subject of my next exposé. The result was a wave of lowered eyes and hushed whispers as I made my way to class.

On a positive note, it made getting to fourth period easier.

It was only the second week of school, but the harassment of Freshman Initiation was already in full swing. This Monday morning, it was a couple members of the offensive line who'd cornered some unsuspecting kid against the lockers and were in the process of giving him a wedgie that would require a proctologist to remove. The fear in his eyes matched his sheet-white face as guys who weighed twice as much as him hauled his underwear out of his jeans.

I snapped a picture of the scene with my phone. Then I moved behind the hulking mass of muscle and fat and tapped one of them on the shoulder. "Hey, I know steroids can cause your penis to shrink, but is that really a reason to take it out on a stranger?"

The one I tapped spun around, his hand clenching and unclenching in a fist as though he were about to dole out the same underwear-tugging punishment to me. He froze statue-still when he realized he was messing with the Queen B.

"I'm thinking about writing an article on steroid-induced aggression," I continued in a casual manner snapping another picture that included his face. "What do you think? Would you like to do an interview?"

His lax-jawed expression mirrored the dull lack of intelligence in his eyes. He nudged his buddy and uttered a few caveman grunts. His friend turned around, and for a split second, the fear in his face matched that of their victim. They dumped the freshman and took a step toward me.

I stood my ground, emailing the pictures to myself in case

things got out of hand.

I'd barely managed to hit send before Caveman #1 snatched my phone away from me. "I'm not ending up on your blog."

"Break my phone if you want. I've already loaded the pictures to my cloud." I crossed my arms and tried to look cool, even though my pulse was running a bit higher than usual. One thing I'd learned over the years during my rise to Queen B status was never to let them know how much control they had. "Besides, I can add destruction of property to my roid-rage article."

His beefy hand curled around my phone, and I imagined him wanting to shatter the glad screen. But before he got to that point, his friend nudged him. "Don't piss her off, dude. Remember what she did to Jamal."

Caveman #1 replied with a pig-like snort, but he returned my phone. "We weren't doing anything wrong. Just teaching the Fresh Meat here about Eastline traditions."

He took another step toward me, his foot stomping against the tile floor.

The freshman jumped, and I answered only with an arched brow. I knew I had the upper hand, especially with pictures to prove it.

A staring match followed for another ten seconds before he turned and disappeared down the hall.

"Thank you so much," the freshman said in a quivering voice. He bent down to pick up his scattered books, looking up at me like I was some kind of superhero.

It required me to turn my Queen B glare on him too. Sorry, but very few people got on my good list, and this kid wasn't going to be one of them. "Numbskulls like them feed off fear, and until you grow a set of balls or find wedgie-proof underwear, I'd suggest you find a group of fellow freshmen and travel in packs."

Some small part of me felt pity for the kid, but he needed to learn the hard truth if he wanted to survive Eastline High. Besides, I had a one good deed a day limit. Otherwise, I'd get a reputation for being nice.

I made my way to my last class of the morning, one of those stupid required-for-graduation courses I'd postponed as long as possible. *Optimizing the Human Experience.* As if making me sit through this puffed-up health class would affect my future.

It was considered a joke class up until this year. I'd even written a piece on my blog about how easy it was to breeze through. If you had a pulse and showed up to class, you got an A. Unfortunately, over the summer the school board had outfitted the classroom with technology more suitable for the offspring of Microsoft millionaires and revamped the class to make it more challenging. The teacher actually gave homework now, and based on this weekend's assignment, I dreaded what some of the juvenile reactions to today's topic might be.

Of course, it would helpful if I could actually get into the classroom.

My nemesis, Summer Hoyt—head cheerleader and this year's Queen Bee—was stationed with her court at the door. The overindulged daughter of a coffee-chain magnate and a Hong Kong real estate heiress, she paraded around campus like a Homecoming Queen Barbie, plastic parts included (because there was no way she went from an A-cup to a C naturally over winter break last year).

Perfect highlights in her dark brown hair? Check. Immaculately groomed brows and manicured nails? Check.

Hours spent at the tanning salon so she could have a sprayed-on golden glow that made people wonder if she lived in LA rather than Seattle? Check. Attitude that could rival a supermodel? But of course.

Summer was the only person in the school who thought she could still get to me. Failing miserably every time, I might add, but she kept trying. Maybe it had something to do with the fact that once upon a time, we'd been best friends.

At the moment, she was practically draped over Brett Pederson, the star quarterback, and was talking to him in this low, breathy voice. "Why don't we have a little fun under the bleachers at lunch?"

I thought I might hurl if I was forced to watch or listen to this for long.

"Excuse me, but can you two get a room?" I pushed my way between them. "I'd like to get to my seat on time."

Summer narrowed her eyes and gave me a tight smile. Part of me briefly remembered when we'd practically been inseparable. She'd been the one person I'd trust all my secrets to. But that was before we graduated to junior high. Before she became a cheerleader and learned that in order to hold her place at the top of the pyramid, she needed to trample those under her.

Before she betrayed me by stealing the diary from my bedroom and reading all my hopes and fears aloud to everyone in the cafeteria on the first day of sixth grade.

Summer placed her hand on her jutted-out hip. "Jealous, Alexis?"

"Please, I just threw up a little in my mouth. I thought this was high school, not a strip club giving out free lap dances. Are you trying to attract customers with your new boobs? I bet Daddy used them as a tax write-off."

Brett, to his credit, coughed and turned away, but not before I caught the grin he tried to hide. He almost looked relieved to be free of the Summer-puppet dangling around his neck.

Summer opened her mouth, but Brett took her arm and murmured, "Leave her alone unless you want to end up on her blog," soothing her as well as any snake charmer.

I rolled my eyes and moved to my seat in the back of the room. Because Eastline was in the Tesla-filled suburbs of Seattle, the school had decided to do away with individual desks and installed three-person tables with charging stations for laptops and tablets. An unwise sophomore sat at my preferred spot, typing away on his laptop. I banged my books down next to him and gave him what my best friend, Morgan, called my "eat shit and die" look.

The sophomore's face paled. He scooped up his belongings and backed away from me so quickly, he tripped on his shoelaces and crashed into an empty chair.

I haven't needed to share my space since I'd publicly called out the junior sitting next to me for peeking at my answers during finals my sophomore year.

The bell rang, and the students who'd been loitering outside the classroom tumbled in to take their seats. I steepled my fingers under my chin, daring any of them to sit beside me.

None did.

Another perk of being the Queen B.

Mr. DePaul stepped out from behind his desk. "Settle down, everyone. As you probably guessed from the weekend's homework, we're going to start the unit on reproduction. Normally, we would begin with the birds and the bees and how not to get knocked up."

One of the football players snickered.

"But the school board is suddenly debating whether teaching you about condom use is acceptable." Mr. DePaul dragged a pair of large plastic bins from the closet. "So I've decided to start with the consequences of unprotected sex."

It was probably a little too late for that. I suspected half the football team already had herpes. Perhaps that would be the subject of my next blog post.

He opened the bin and pulled out a doll. "Students, meet your babies."

Ah. Children, the STD that keeps on living even after you're dead. The entire class groaned.

"Since it takes two of you to make one of these little bundles of joy, I'm going to be pairing you off. Today we're going to do a little exercise in genetics, and tomorrow, you'll receive your babies. For the next two weeks, you're going to be parents."

The muscles in my shoulders tensed into knots as he tucked the doll back into the bin. Marvelous. I hated group assignments, especially when I couldn't choose my partner. I always ended up doing all the work. I refused to let my class rank suffer because of someone else's laziness. As the person holding the highest class ranking at the end of last year, I was on track to being valedictorian, and no one was going to take that title away from me. I had nine months left in this level of hell that Dante missed, and then I would be free to move on to whatever Ivy League school I wanted to attend.

"We have an equal number of guys and girls in the class, so it should be easy to pair everyone up," Mr. DePaul continued.

"But what if I want to be gay with my teammates and be part of a same-sex couple?" Sanchez, ever the smartass, asked. He laughed and exchanged high-fives with another football player.

"If the school board won't let me teach you about condoms, you know they won't allow gay marriage in the classroom, even though it's legal here. If you want a class in that kind of lifestyle, move to Capitol Hill." Mr. DePaul snatched the baseball cap off of Sanchez's head and held it out. "Ladies, if you'll be so kind as to enter your names into the drawing."

I scribbled my name on a piece of paper, each stroke of my pen adding to my annoyance. I glanced at the potential fathers and deemed them all unfit. My gaze lingered on Brett a second longer than the others. Well, maybe not all of them, but none of them met my standards. All high school boys seemed to care about was scoring, both on and off the field. Way too immature for me. The last few dates I'd been on over the summer had been with college guys, and even they got on my nerves.

As I sauntered to the front of the class and dropped my name in the hat, I couldn't resist the temptation to exert my power as a Queen B. I grinned and squeezed my thumb and index fingers close together until they were about an inch apart, all while mouthing the word *tiny* at Sanchez. Much to my delight, he lowered his eyes, and the tips of his ear turned red. I laughed quietly all the way back to my seat.

After all the girls had put their names in, Mr. DePaul walked around the room with the hat to let the guys draw their partners. When he came to Sanchez, the star wide receiver glanced at me and made the sign of the cross before pulling out a piece of paper. His body sagged in relief when he read the name on it.

I sighed in relief, too. The last thing I wanted was to be paired up with that bonehead.

"Now that everyone has been paired off, let's get to work

on the genetics." He gave the hat back to Sanchez and started placing a handful of Popsicle sticks in front of each girl.

The guys milled around, each one finding his "mate." As I waited to see who I was stuck with, I drummed my fingers on my table. I reminded myself it was just a school project and would be over in a couple of weeks. It wasn't like I'd be stuck with this person for the rest of the semester.

As luck would have it, I ended up with Brett Pederson standing in front of me.

"You're not going to rip me a new one if I venture into your territory?" he asked, not waiting for me to answer before plopping down in the empty chair to my right.

My normal response would've been to tell him to piss off, but for some strange reason, my throat constricted. He smelled good. I mean really good, like he'd soaked in some sort of pheromone bath. My stomach started fluttering. I felt like one of those brainless twits in a cologne commercial who was drawn to the guy simply because of his scent.

Stupid teenage hormones.

I coughed to clear both my mind and my throat. "Why bother asking if you're going to do what you want?"

He shrugged and took the Popsicle sticks from Mr. DePaul. "I can't work with you from across the room."

"Ah, so you're the fortunate jock who drew my name from the hat?" Great. That meant I was going to end up doing everything, just as I'd suspected.

"You don't have to be so sarcastic." He divided the sticks up between us. "I want an A as much as you do. I'm willing to pull my weight."

How refreshing. Complete bullshit, but refreshing.

Mr. DePaul was back at the front of the class before I could comment on Brett's desire for fair and equal work. "If you pull up your assignments from this weekend, I asked you to answer some questions about you and your family."

Two dozen laptops and tablets flared to life, including mine. I stared at the information I'd put in. Blue eyes. Light brown hair, curly. No mid-digital hair on my fingers. No mental disorders, unless you counted the fact that my younger sister, Taylor, was a cheerleader. No bleeding disorders. No cystic fibrosis. No cancers. All and all, pretty boring stuff.

"Now, if you click the 'Give Me My Genes' button, it will give you the alleles for your genetic information," Mr. DePaul continued. "Please put this information on the sticks I've given you, one allele on each side. Once that's done, you and your partner will drop your genes and create a baby using whatever alleles land face up on the floor. Yes, I know it's low tech, but I have to make sure you're working the entire period."

I didn't miss the accusing glance Mr. DePaul sent my way with the last sentence.

"I'd much rather drop my other jeans and make a baby that way," Sanchez muttered from the table next to us, earning a smack across the back of his head from Brett.

I tried to squelch the little surge of admiration for Brett that suddenly rose inside me. Instead, I bent over my sticks, focusing on my assignment. I finished before my partner did and risked leaning in a little closer just to get a second sniff of him.

Yeah, he still smelled good.

He caught me out of the corner of his eye. "Something wrong, Lexi?"

I instantly prickled. "No one calls me that."

"Taylor does."

"She's my sister. Therefore, she's exempt from my wrath."

His eyes crinkled when he smiled. "But not me, eh?"

"Not even close." I crossed my arms over my chest and stared at my computer screen. "I was just checking to make sure you didn't have any worrisome alleles."

"Nope. Both my parents are in excellent health."

Which probably explained his outstanding genetics. I would willingly admit that Brett was pleasing in the looks department. Maybe even a little bit hot. He was six feet tall, lean and muscular with black hair, chocolaty brown eyes, and lashes my sister would pay good money for. He was tanned, too, although he appeared to have that rich coppery glow year-round. And he had to be somewhat intelligent because I'd seen him at Honor Society meetings.

But he still was a jock, and the fact he was dating Summer made me deduct thirty-plus points in my overall rating of him.

He finished labeling the last of his sticks and gathered them in his hands. "Ready?"

"I suppose, if we must." I followed his lead and dropped my sticks on the floor.

"I'll call out the alleles, and you enter them in the program." He bent over, organizing the genetic traits one by one. He waited until the end before announcing proudly that the Y chromosome had reared its ugly head. He held up the Popsicle stick with a proud grin. "Congratulations! We're having a boy!"

"Oh, joy," I said flatly, typing in that result a bit harder than normal. "There go half of his brain cells to testosterone."

Brett drew his dark brows together and studied me. "Do you not like guys or something?"

"Are you suggesting I don't?"

"Well, the only guy I've ever seen you be nice to is Richard Wang, and let's face it, he's definitely not in the closet about his sexual orientation."

My cheeks burned. "Just because one of my best friends is gay doesn't necessarily mean I am," I replied, hoping to God no one else was listening to this conversation.

"So you're just an über-feminist or something, huh?"

"You say that like it's a bad thing." I added the "shut the hell up" edge to my voice that usually ended any conversation, but Brett was either too oblivious to catch the hint or completely immune to my Queen B powers.

"Well, you've been known to deliver a good kick to the balls with just a look."

"Would you rather I deliver the real thing?"

"Please don't—I don't need half the team on the injured roster this Friday."

I rolled my eyes and focused on saving our information into a file to email to Mr. DePaul so we'd get credit for this part of the project. Words were my weapons, not physical violence. "Is there a point to this conversation?"

"I was just curious," he said with a shrug. "Besides, I needed to know if I should be wearing my cup for the next two weeks."

My lips twitched, much to my dismay. I should be pissed off that he was poking fun at me. I should be reinforcing my reputation as the Queen B of the school. But something about Brett intrigued me. He was the first person in a long time who actually seemed impervious to my barbs.

Time to rectify that. "I doubt you have much to protect."

"Ow, that was a zinger," he said with a mocking wince. "I expected better from you, Lexi."

I balled my hands into fists, fighting the uncharacteristic yearning to whack him. My usual go-to weapons wouldn't work because Brett transferred to Eastline sophomore year. I had nothing to throw at him, no embarrassing leverage. It didn't help that he was the school's golden boy. Nothing stuck to him. If there were any skeletons in his closet, they were well hidden. As far as I knew, he was perfect.

Well, except for the Summer thing.

"I don't want to waste my energy on you," I finally said, realizing how lame it sounded as soon as the words left my mouth.

He had the gall to grin as he leaned over close enough to where I could feel his warm breath on my cheek. "Your panties are in a wad because I'm not scared of you."

My pulse jumped to a sprint, and my palms started to sweat. "You should be," I replied, my voice not nearly as threatening as I wanted it to be.

Brett laughed as the bell rang, snapping his laptop closed and joining his friends.

I sat there, willing my body to stop shaking. I had to pull myself together, to put my game face on before wading into the masses. I was about to throw my things into my bag when I noticed a folded slip of paper from his backpack had fluttered to the ground. I picked up the slip and read the name of another girl in the class.

Brett hadn't drawn my name from the hat.

Two questions immediately popped into my head. One: which guy had drawn my name in the first place and was too chicken-shit to work with me?

And two: why had Brett switched places with him?

15

"Who wants some extra credit? Lydia Montego, that's who. Look how cozy she is sitting in Mr. Rodchenko's lap.
A = lap dance in that algebra class."

The Eastline Spy
May, Sophomore Year

Chapter 2

"So, I heard some juicy gossip about you," Richard Wang, the most flamboyantly gay guy this side of Capitol Hill, said as I collapsed under the large maple tree near the football field. We first met a couple years ago when he was getting harassed by some upperclassmen and I intervened. I admired his ability to be comfortable with himself and to be openly out when most teens kept quiet about their sexuality, and we'd been friends ever since.

My best friend, Morgan, joined us. Inked and pierced in multiple places thanks to her fake ID, she was determined to be the antithesis of Abercrombie and Fitch. "Spill."

Richard beamed now that he had an audience and sat down on the grass. "It seems our dear little Alexis here procreated with Brett Pederson."

Morgan's jaw dropped. "Please tell me you were suffering from a temporary bout of insanity, Miss 'Nobody Is Good

Enough To Get Between My Legs.' "

"It's not what you think." I pulled my tablet out of my bag and checked my storyboard. As the creator of a weekly blog that had exposed more than one scandal at Eastline, it was my job to make sure I had something that would get people to read and react. "We're just paired up for a project in Mr. DePaul's Hum-Ex class."

"Oh, the 'Dropping Your Genes' project," Morgan said with a snicker, twirling her finger in the air as if to say "big whoop." "You have my deepest sympathies."

"Not mine." Richard bumped my shoulder with his. "I'd love to have some one-on-one time with Mr. Quarterback. Maybe I'd even teach him a few new plays of my own."

"I doubt you could convert him to the other team." That quivering returned to my stomach as I thought about how good Brett smelled. Time to change the subject. "Richard, any updates on that sex discrimination story?"

"I'd much rather focus on a sexual story with your project partner."

"This is a newspaper, not an issue of *Playgirl*."

"It's Play*guy*, and fine, I'll live out my fantasies in my own head. At least one of us isn't completely hung up on stereotypes." He got up and crossed the campus in a huff, flicking off every blade of grass that would dare stick to his jeans.

Morgan, however, lingered under the tree with me. "Don't sweat it. It's just two weeks. The worst part will be handling the switch-offs for child care."

"Meaning I'll probably be stuck with the kid the whole time."

She shook her head. "These are top-of-the-line fake babies that record everything. You have to enter in a code when you have it. Then, it cries when it's wet or hungry or teething—"

"So in other words, I'm not going to be sleeping much during the next two weeks."

"Yeah, pretty much." She started playing with the tiny barbell in her eyebrow. "But since we're on the subject of hot guys—"

"I never said Brett was hot," I said loud enough for anyone within ten feet of us to overhear. "I'm just paired up with him for a class project, nothing more."

"And I know you better than that. He must have done something to get under your skin."

I weighed the risk of confiding about my body's undesired reaction to him, but decided against it in case anyone around us was listening in on the conversation. "He switched places with someone to work with me," I mumbled.

"Okay, now I'm thinking *he* must be the one suffering a temporary bout of insanity." I pressed my lips together, and she added, "Not that I don't love you and all, but you have the tendency to go a little bat-crazy when it comes to class projects."

"I demand perfection from myself, and I'd hope my partners will give it their best efforts as well."

"Yes, but we're seniors now, so you can stop cracking the whip. Anyway, back to hot guys. You should come to The Purple Dog with me and see the new guy working there. Without the baby, though."

The Purple Dog was a café in the U-District. Morgan liked to hang out there because it was frequented by university students and, therefore, was far more "intelligent" than the local hangouts. "What? Scared the new guy will freak out when he realizes we're still in high school?"

"Speak for yourself. I've been taking college classes since

last year."

Morgan was enrolled in Running Start, a program that allowed high school students to take classes at a local community college for college credit. She liked to rub in the fact she was at college while I'd chosen to stay in high school and take AP classes to maintain my class rank. That didn't change the fact she was seventeen and needed a fake ID to even get a tattoo.

I jumped on the opportunity to talk about something other than Brett. "So tell me about him. How many piercings does he have?"

"None."

"Tattoos?" I didn't bother asking about the eyeliner, since that was usually on Morgan's list of musts.

"None that I can see."

My eyes widened. "Who are you, and what have you done with my best friend?"

She laughed. "I know, right? He's not my type, which is why I'm wondering why I'm attracted to him. But he has this cool, laid-back vibe about him that has me wondering if he's always that way in every situation. And he seemed really into me this weekend."

"Into you, or in you?" Most people who met Morgan saw her as a pessimistic, snarky goth girl who sometimes bordered on nymphomaniac. I'd lost count of how many hookups she'd had in the last year. But she handled sex with far more maturity than most people and didn't seem to form any attachments to the guys she slept with. For her, it was purely physical.

And maybe a way to get back at her ultraconservative parents.

She laughed again, a dreamy look filling her eyes as she twirled her dyed-black hair around her finger. This was the real

19

Morgan, the one who carefully hid her inner romantic behind her tough-girl exterior. "No, not yet. But if he offered, I wouldn't say no."

"And another man falls victim to the Queen of Darkness."

"So, what are you going to do about your project partner?"

I took a deep breath to collect myself. We were back to Brett again. "I'm going to interact with him as little as possible."

"Methinks the lady doth protest too much. If it were me, I'd do him just to piss Summer off," Morgan whispered before standing up and heading toward the parking lot.

At least she'd provided me with one silver lining to all this. For the next two weeks, Brett would be working side by side with me, which would drive Summer nuts.

***

"Oh my God! My life is over!"

My sister's wail barely fazed me. I heard the exact same exclamation from Taylor at least once a week. I sighed and went back to reading my well-worn copy of *The Taming of the Shrew*, having finished my homework hours ago. For some reason, that book was calling to me.

My lack of response apparently didn't please her. She ran into my room with her MacBook Air and shoved the screen in my face. "Look at this, Lexi."

The fuzzy images from the YouTube clip played for about five seconds before I realized what I was looking at. The overly tanned skin. The excess of enhanced blondes. The fake giggles. "Who's been filming the cheerleading squad in the locker room?"

Taylor thrust her bottom lip out in a pout. "I don't know, but my reputation is ruined. Now everyone will know I use inserts in my bra."

Just as she said that, I saw the meat of the film — all the cheerleaders stripping off their underwear to hit the showers. I slammed the laptop shut. "Aren't you upset that people are watching you naked?"

Her brows furrowed together as if that thought had never crossed her airhead mind. I'm pretty sure all that "Ra Ra Sisboom-ba" shit involved with cheerleading must have caused some brain damage. Either that or all the sunless tanner she applied to give her a glow that only an Oompa Loompa could call natural had seeped into her skull. "I mean, I suppose I should be upset about that," she said slowly, but then added in a rush, "but now they'll see how small my boobs really are."

I drew a deep breath and counted to ten while I fought off the urge to shake some sense into her. I gave up hope a long time ago that Taylor would develop into a woman of substance. Instead, she focused on the here and now, the superficial, and had only one goal in life—to become head cheerleader.

I held up the laptop. "This is an invasion of your privacy. Some guy has probably been jacking off while watching you and the rest of the cheerleaders prance around naked for months."

"You're right!" The anger I'd been waiting to see finally flashed in her blue eyes. "Some nerd is looking at my perfect ass. As if!"

She whipped out her phone and began texting at a rate that would put a professional transcriptionist to shame. "I'm going to tell Summer about this."

"It would probably be a better idea to remove the camera if it's still there." I turned back to my book.

She paused. "Oh, that would be a good idea."

Her phone buzzed, and she checked her message.

"Summer agrees that we should do something about it. Where do you think the camera is, though?"

When I didn't answer, she yanked the book from my hands. "Hello? I'm having a bit of a crisis here."

"If you watch the video, you can probably figure out where it is." I wasn't going to get involved with this drama. Even though I did have a sick feeling in my stomach at the idea of someone violating the sanctity of the girls' locker room, I was more sick at the idea that discovering the culprit would help Summer. It was about time someone knocked her down a notch or two. She'd been full of herself for as long as I'd known her, and now that we were seniors, she'd become completely insufferable. She needed to get her comeuppance.

I tried to grab my book back, but Taylor held it up out of my reach. "Please. You don't want video porn of your little sister out there for everyone to see, do you?"

"It's not porn." I paused. Who knew what games those girls played after practice? "Unless you're into chicks."

"No, that would be Alyssa and Emma," she replied, full of sarcasm, "but they broke up once they sobered up."

Ooh, another story idea. Booze-induced cheerleader on cheerleader action.

But her plea spoke to something deep inside me and helped me focus on what was important. She was my little sister, after all. I had to look out for her because she obviously couldn't look out for herself. "Fine, I'll check out the locker room tomorrow morning and see if I can find it."

"Thank you!" She threw her arms around me in a hug. "I promise I won't tell anyone you agreed to help."

"You're so kind."

"Well, I know you want to maintain your reputation for being a cruel bitch." She looked at my book and scanned the page. "Why do you keep reading this?"

"Because I happen to enjoy it. If you tried reading every once in a while, you might find it's something you enjoy, too."

She tossed the book on the bed as if it was an out-of-style pair of jeans. "I *have* read a book. In fact, I read three of them last year."

Her smug expression almost had me doubled over in laughter. I'd easily read thirty times that in the past year.

"Oh, yes, that series with the doormat idiot of a girl. Really stimulating reading." I found my place again and tried to lose myself in the third act.

"At least she had a boyfriend instead of being the biggest man-repellent in the school. And speaking of boyfriends, Summer told me to tell you to keep your hands off hers."

"Trust me, there is no danger of me touching Brett Pederson." Smelling him was an entirely different matter. "And it's refreshing to know that Summer's so insecure about her relationship with Brett that she has to send threats through her little minions."

"I'm not her minion, whatever that is. And she's not threatened at all by you. She just wants to make sure you know where you stand." Taylor stomped out of my room, leaving her laptop behind.

As hard as I wanted to continue reading, the more I thought about the video, the more irritated I became. I popped open the computer and replayed the video. I'd probably need to stab a couple of hot pokers in my eyes to purge some of those images from my mind, but by the end, I had a good idea where the camera was located.

Now, if only I could discover the person behind it.

"Did you hear about this year's joke class? If you have a pulse, you'll get an A in 'Health'. No wonder the entire football team is taking it this semester."

The Eastline Spy
September, Junior Year

Chapter 3

Thanks to Taylor's eyeliner *emergency*, we barely made it to school on time. The argument that began in the car ended with her slamming the door of my Prius after telling me she'd be getting a ride from someone less anal than me from now on.

I didn't have time to inspect the locker room until midmorning break. It was thankfully empty when I walked in. A few seconds later, I spied the desktop camera sitting on top of the lockers. I snapped a towel toward it, knocking it onto the ground. It had a small antenna, but no plug, no source of power. I turned it over, searching for any clues about its owner, before turning it back to me.

"Listen, asshole," I said into the lens, pouring every ounce of Queen Bitchiness into my voice, "I'm on to you, and you don't want to piss me off any more than you already have. Take those videos down, or else."

Then I tossed the camera into one of the feminine hygiene

bins, doubting whoever was behind the videos would wade through the sea of tampons to retrieve it.

Mission accomplished.

I was actually feeling pretty good until I ran into Summer in the hallway. She got in my face, one perfectly manicured claw inches from my nose. "Taylor told me what you said, so I'm going to deliver this message in person. Stay away from Brett."

I was so tempted to tell her he'd been the one who'd chosen to work with me, but until I knew the reason why, I was keeping that to myself. Instead, I would have to be content to push her buttons in other ways. I swatted her hand away. "Sorry, Summer, but we're going to have to work together very closely for the next two weeks. After all, we are sharing a baby."

Her face turned red. "He's mine."

"So you think."

She froze, and a look flashed across her face as though she finally realized she was falling right into my trap. The laughter that followed sounded tight and false. "What am I worried about? What chance does someone like you have with him, especially when he has me?"

I lifted my chest, fully aware of how my T-shirt clung to my bust. "Maybe he's tired of playing with silicone parts."

Summer glanced down at my *au naturel* size Cs and scowled.

"Now, if you'll excuse me, I have to get to Calculus." I stepped around her, moving on before the Queen Bee had given me permission to leave.

I didn't need her permission for anything.

***

My skin tingled as Brett slid into the seat next to me. "I need your phone number," he said as the bell rang.

My stomach dropped in a free fall of panic. "Why?"

"In case I want to hook up sometime," he whispered, grinning.

The air burned in my lungs but refused to move.

His grin widened. "Just kidding. I was thinking it would be useful in arranging handoffs for the baby."

Unfortunately, Brett's conversation had caught Mr. DePaul's attention. "What's so important that you're holding up class, Mr. Pederson?"

"I was just trying to get Alexis's digits," he announced to the class, which erupted into snickers.

How many days would I be suspended for giving the star quarterback a black eye?

I pretended to read something on my laptop, rage simmering just beneath my skin. Forget any shreds of respect I might have had for Brett. He and Summer deserved each other.

"Your social activities can wait until after class." He pulled out the bin of babies again. "Okay, today we're going to go over the intricacies of the dolls you'll be carrying around for the next two weeks. Let's start with the need for you to be very gentle with them, not only because real babies are delicate, but because these are sensitive pieces of equipment that run about nine hundred dollars a pop. If you break one of them, you'll not only get an F, you'll also get a bill. Are we clear?"

He waited until most of the class nodded. "Now that we've laid down the most basic rule, come up and get your doll and your project codes."

Brett got ours and brought it back to the table, fascinated by the miniature computer disguised as a baby. He pointed to an unnatural opening on the doll's back. "USB drive. This must be where DePaul gets the information from at the end

26

of the project."

Before I could ask him to explain that, Mr. DePaul launched into an hour long lecture about the doll. How to turn it on. How to enter the project code assigned to us so we'd get credit for our time with the baby. How to simulate feeding and changing. How it was important to charge the doll every night. With every requirement, my anxiety rose a bit more, especially since he was ending each section with, "Failure to do so will result in an F."

I eyed the doll with a mixture of wariness and resentment. My class rank would not suffer because of this stupid project.

"What's wrong?" Brett asked, taking notes while he continued to look at the PowerPoint presentation in the front of the class.

"I'm not very maternal."

"No shit."

"Aren't you worried about screwing up and failing?"

He shook his head. "I have three little sisters. Been there, done that as far as babies are concerned."

Thank God one of us had a clue what to do with this doll. "So you're going to show me how to change a diaper, right?"

"Why don't you ask your mother to teach you?"

"She's too busy ridding the Eastside of acne and wrinkles."

The corner of his mouth twitched. "Your dad?"

"Too busy screwing his latest graduate assistant."

Then he turned to me with the one thing I never wanted to see in his eyes—pity. "Broken home?"

"Fuck you."

He laughed softly. He'd just managed to get under my skin again and exposed a weakness, and he knew it. "Okay, I'll show you how to change a diaper, but on one condition."

I dreaded to ask what, and he didn't wait for me to respond.

"You have baby duty today."

And so it begins—super jock was already trying to dump the project on me. "Why?"

"Because I need time to bribe my sister to babysit. You take the baby today, and in the morning, we can switch off, twenty-four hours at a time. Sound fair?"

I looked at the doll, still hearing Mr. DePaul threatening to give an F even though he'd stopped talking a couple of minutes ago. "Your sister is old enough to babysit?"

"She's thirteen and helps take care of the two younger ones all the time."

I wasn't quite convinced. Taylor was fifteen, and there was no way in hell I'd let her near this doll.

"You're going to have to trust me on this, Lexi."

"Don't call me that."

"Fine," he said with an exaggerated sigh. "The alternative is me taking Junior here to practice and hoping he doesn't get tackled or mistaken for a football."

"Your sister will work," I said in a rush as I visualized Sanchez tossing the baby in the air and breaking it. Then I caught something in his words that I'd missed before. "So you're not going to make me do all the work?"

"Fat chance. I want an A, and if DePaul finds out I'm not pulling my share of the work, I'm not getting it."

I cocked my head to the side, trying to decide if I believed his bullshit or not.

"By the way, I brought something from home that you might find helpful." He pulled a black contraption from his backpack. "This is an infant carrier—very useful when you want to keep your hands free while carrying the baby."

I tried to make sense of all the straps and fasteners, but after a few seconds, I was completely lost. I gritted my teeth.

I would have to ask Brett for help. "How does it work?"

"Here, I'll show you." He looped two of the straps around my shoulders and snapped them into place. "The X goes in the back, and the pouch goes in the front like so. Then, you put the baby here and lock into place."

Five seconds later, the doll was pressed against my chest, and Brett was conveniently helping it rest its head comfortably on my boobs. And much to my horror, I kind of liked him standing this close to me, touching that part of my body. It was far from actual groping, but every little brush of his fingers sent a little shiver through me. I was running dangerously close to giving into my hormones and letting him continue.

I slapped his hands away before it was too late. "Hands off!"

He backed away, hands up in front of him. "What? You have a nice rack." His gaze lingered on that part of my anatomy. "In fact, I'm a little envious of Junior there."

"I can't believe you just said that." I turned around and tried adjusting the doll so it wasn't being smothered in my cleavage. The reprieve also gave me a moment to pull myself together. My cheeks were still burning from the realization that I was suffering from a bad case of Brett-itis. "Actually, I can. You're a bonehead jock who's too busy thinking with his dick."

"God gave men both a brain and a penis and only enough blood to use one at a time," he replied matter-of-factly.

"Well, start thinking with your other head before I take the lower one out of commission."

"And we're back to the ball-busting." The amused glint in his dark brown eyes told me he'd witnessed my moment of weakness, that he saw the flush that still lingered in my face (and other parts of my body I refused to acknowledge). "So, back to getting your phone number…"

I closed my eyes to clear my head. "Just for exchanges, right?"

"Sure, if that's what you want."

"Yes." So far, every conversation I'd had with Brett ended with me alternating between wanting to punch him in the face or jump his bones.

"No worries." When I opened my eyes, he was focused on his phone. "Anytime now."

I gave him my number, which he entered into his contacts. Part of me wanted to snicker. How pissed off would Summer be once she discovered my number in his phone?

"Do you want my number?" he asked when he was done.

"Kind of hard to get to my phone with this doll strapped to my chest."

His eyes flickered to my chest again. This time, I managed to limit my response to pure annoyance and snapped my fingers in front of his face. "Eyes up here, bucko."

"Fine, let me write it down for you." He tore a scrap of paper off something in his backpack and scribbled his number on it. He pressed it into my palm, reviving that irritating shiver I got every time he touched me. "I'm sure you're just dying to conveniently misplace this, but please wait until after the project is done."

The slip of paper reminded me of the one I found yesterday, but the bell rang before I could confront him about that. He was gone, and I was left with an eight-pound computerized doll and a growing sense of confusion when it came to Brett Pederson.

***

One perk about having enough credits to only have to go to school for half a day was that I could leave at lunch and not be subjected to what the cafeteria called food while surrounded by a bunch of adolescent idiots.

Which was perfect because Junior started screaming in the car on the way home.

My shoulders tightened, and my knuckles turned white on the steering wheel as I was forced to listen for almost two miles. I was a frazzled set of nerves by the time I pulled into the driveway and rushed inside, setting the doll on the kitchen counter. "What's wrong with you?" I asked it, silently wishing a message would scroll across its face telling me exactly what to do.

Instead, I was left to figure it out on my own. The doll had come with one reusable diaper, and I vaguely remembered Mr. DePaul saying we had to remove it and replace it to simulate a diaper change. Two minutes later, I think I had it back on the right way, but Junior was still screaming its electronic head off.

"Bottle," I whispered, rummaging through my bag for the fake bottle with the sensor built into the tip. "Let me just stick a bottle in his mouth and pray it works."

Thank God it did. The electronic crying turned into sucking and cooing, indicating a happy baby.

Too bad I didn't share its contentment. I slumped against the kitchen counter and held the bottle in the doll's mouth until the noises stopped.

If Eastline High wanted to discourage teen pregnancy, their point was well taken. I was going straight to my family doc and demanding to be put on the pill pronto, even though having sex was the furthest thing from my mind right now.

Of course, the minute I thought about sex, that little flopping in my stomach that appeared every time I was near Brett returned, the unwelcome little nuisance. I needed a date with someone the exact opposite of Brett Pederson. Someone mature, intelligent, politically correct.

Oh, screw that. I just needed a good old-fashioned make out session with someone.

Just not him. He was way too dangerous for my liking.

I pulled out my phone and dialed Morgan. "Do you want to hang out at The Purple Dog tomorrow?"

"I dunno," she replied. "Will you have the doll with you?"

"Nope. Brett said he was going to hire his sister to babysit. I'll be childless."

"Awesome!" Her voice perked up. "I'll introduce you to Gavin, and then you can tell me what you think about him."

"And Gavin is Mr. Tattoo-less?"

"I never said he didn't have tattoos—just none that I could see. I'm sure if I got him naked, I might be pleasantly surprised."

"Time out. You just met him this weekend, and you're already talking about getting him naked?"

"I've been going through a dry spell," she countered, a pout coming through the airwaves. "The last time I got laid was July at Lake Chelan."

"Two months is such a *long* dry spell." I eyed the quiet doll, thanking my lucky stars that my virginal status meant I wasn't in danger of contracting one of those. "Speaking of which, who did you hook up with down there?"

"Just some hottie I met on the lake." I could see her giving a nonchalant shrug as she said it. "He liked my piercings and could do wicked things with his tongue."

"Please stop. I don't need the visuals." Especially since I had a pretty good idea which piercings she was referring to.

"You sound like you could use a good boink-fest. Should I see if Gavin has a friend to take away your V-card?"

My gaze drifted back to the doll again. "No, thank you."

"Fine. Then tell me this—did you give Brett your number?"

I let my forehead fall to the granite countertop. Despite the initial whack, the cold stone soothed my pounding head. "Are there any secrets in our school?"

"Not when it comes to this whole you and Brett thing. The entire school is talking about it. And you should've seen the shit-fit Summer had when she found out about the phone number request."

"First, there is no 'me and Brett thing.' " A little wiggle of disappointment nagged my gut as I said that. Even though he epitomized everything that was wrong with the social hierarchy in high school, I kept getting little glimpses of the person who hid behind the role of star quarterback. It was a person who intrigued me. "We're just working together for a class project—"

"That he switched places with someone to work with you on."

"Which I still have no idea why." And was precisely one of the reasons I couldn't easily dismiss him as the bonehead jock.

"Maybe he's harboring a secret crush for you," Morgan said in an overly dramatic tone, complete with the "duh-duh-DUH" at the end.

I thought back to the way he kept checking out my chest this morning before getting the "you're being delusional" wake-up call. "He's dating Summer."

"Yeah, that does put a kink in my theory. He's probably trying to get dirt on you so he can pass it on to her in exchange for sex."

I tried to laugh it off. "You mean she's not dishing it out for free?"

"No way. Girls like Summer use sex as a commodity that will only be given out once the party has met her demands. They end up becoming useless, arm-candy country club wives like my mother. I swear, I think she demands diamonds from my dad before she'll put out."

And I thought my "broken home" was bad. At least my parents split before their dysfunctional relationship made me any more cynical than I already was about romance. "Thanks for the warning, though. I'll be extra careful around him."

"Or you could just try flirting with him and seeing what happens."

"No way. I'm paired up with him until next Friday, and that day can't come soon enough."

"Fine, suit yourself. As for me, I would never turn down a chance to find out what Brett's lips taste like. He's just too yummy."

The granite countertop was no longer soothingly cold, especially after the rush of heat to my face. I lifted my head and massaged my temple with my free hand. "Not tempting enough."

"Liar."

Dammit.

"So are we on for tomorrow or not?" I asked, steering the conversation back to my original question.

"Definitely on! I'll meet you there at two."

Morgan hung up just as Junior started screaming again.

"The 4:20 is still alive and well on campus, but only if you have a medical marijuana card. Just follow your nose to the grove at the end of the football field for your daily dose of vitamin THC."

The Eastline Spy
June, Freshman Year

Chapter 4

I was just dozing off again when my phone rang. I fumbled for it and answered with a groggy "Hello?"

"Good morning." Brett's voice, way too cheerful for this time in the morning, filled the airwaves. "Sounds like you had a rough night."

"I hate you."

"Aw, you shouldn't say that, especially when I'm trying to schedule a time and place to take Junior off your hands."

I lifted my head and cast my bleary-eyed gaze toward my clock.

I had fifteen minutes to get to school.

Shit!

"Alexis, are you there?"

"I slept through my alarm." I jumped out of bed and shimmied out of my pajama pants while holding the phone to my ear.

Brett was laughing on the other end.

"Make it quick," I snapped.

"Fine. I'll meet you by your locker when you get here."

That stopped me cold. "You know where my locker is?"

"Everyone in school knows where your locker is so they can steer clear of it. I'll see you in a bit." He hung up.

I raced around my room, grabbing the first clean shirt I could get my hands on, followed by a pair of jeans. Screw brushing my teeth. I was halfway down the stairs before I realized I'd left the doll up there. I ran back up, snatched the doll from my desk, and ran back downstairs just in time to see Taylor getting into an Audi A4 with gaudy bright teal rims. The car peeled off like the driver was auditioning for one of those drift racing movies.

Must be a guy with a small penis.

At least it meant I wasn't going to be held up because of a makeup emergency today, even though I was worried about my sister making it to school alive.

Parking was a nightmare because I was getting to school so late. I squeezed my Prius into a spot so tiny, I had to hold my breath to get out of the car. If I had a dent in my door by the time I left, I wouldn't be surprised.

The first bell rang as I was running through the front door.

Damn it! I'd never been late to class. Ever. I dashed down the halls to my locker, fully expecting to be stuck with the doll until fourth period, never imagining Brett would've waited for me at the risk of being late himself.

And yet, there he was, leaning against my locker with a cup of coffee.

He grinned at me. "Good morning, Lexi."

"Shut the hell up and take the doll." I shoved it toward him and entered in my combination.

"Someone woke up on the wrong side of bed." He held the cup under my nose, the calming scents of vanilla and hazelnut soothing my ire. "Care for some coffee?"

I took the cup and tasted it. It was perfect. The last of my anger melted away to the point where I almost liked Brett.

Almost.

"How did you know what I usually get?"

"All I had to do was give the barista your name, and she knew exactly what you'd want." He reached into my bag and retrieved the carrier, slipping it on with enviable ease. "It seems you make quite an impression wherever you go."

I took another sip of my coffee to keep from telling him to piss off. It required too much energy, I told myself, when in truth, I figured I could let him off this one time since he waited for me while bearing gifts. "Why did you get me coffee?"

"Because you sounded like you needed it." He pointed to my mirror. "By the way, you might want to do something with your hair. You look like shit."

I knew I'd forgotten to do something this morning. One glimpse of the frizzy mess on top of my head, and a new wave of panic rose into my throat. I dug around my bag to find the hair tie I kept on hand for just such emergencies. A minute later, I'd managed to pull my hair up into a somewhat tame bun.

Brett remained right by my locker, looking at my shirt with a bemused grin.

Uncomfortable warmth crawled up my neck. "What are you waiting for?"

"We're already late, and you still haven't given me the bottle for Junior here."

I pulled it out of my bag, grateful I'd remembered to put it in there during the morning insanity. "Is that all?"

"For now. Love the Monty Python quote, by the way. Very appropriate." His grin widened. "See you in class."

He turned around and continued on to whatever he had for first period.

I glanced down at the shirt I'd put on this morning and groaned as I read it. "Huge Tracts of Land." Lovely. At least he got the reference.

I pulled my emergency hoodie from my locker and zipped it over the quote emblazoned across my chest before heading to class, armed with my large nonfat vanilla hazelnut latte.

By the time fourth period rolled around, I was feeling more like a human being. And as much as I hated to admit it, the coffee helped. When Brett slid into the seat next to me, I mumbled my thanks.

"What was that?" He leaned closer, giving me a good whiff of him.

Yummy, I think was what Morgan called him. I was beginning to agree, at least on some accounts.

"I said thank you for bringing me coffee."

"No worries." He waved the doll's arm at me. "Junior here hopes you're less grouchy now."

"I'm only running on about seventy percent bitch level at the moment. That doll is the spawn of Satan, by the way. It kept screaming every two to three hours last night."

Brett nodded. "Just like a real baby."

"And that doesn't bother you?"

"Nope." He opened up his laptop to begin taking notes. "Try having twins."

"I'd kill myself."

He chuckled. "I'm sure my parents considered that from time to time, but they made it through okay. My sisters are now four."

"You have twin sisters?"

"Yep. Best birds and the bees talk my parents could've ever given me. I'm so not ready for kids."

At least that explained why he was so laid back with this whole fake baby thing. "Just make sure you don't breed with Summer," I said, remembering my conversation with Morgan yesterday.

He turned to me, his brows bunched together and his mouth opening to say something before Mr. DePaul cut him off by jumping into his lecture.

It seems the school board did approve the safe sex lecture because today's PowerPoint was all about STDs and how to use condoms. I glanced around the room to see how many people were squirming in their seats, finally coming to Brett. He was calm and focused on the presentation, his fingers flying over the keys as he took notes.

Probably in preparation for this weekend.

I needed brain bleach every time I thought of him and Summer together.

The bell rang before I realized it. "So, should I bring you coffee tomorrow?" I asked, shocked I'd even offered to act like his personal secretary.

'Nope, hate the stuff." He snapped his laptop closed, the doll still strapped to his chest. "Thanks for offering, though."

***

"He likes you," Morgan said after I'd recounted the whole Brett-coffee incident from this morning.

"Or maybe he was just feeling sorry for me."

She shook her head. "Guys don't do thoughtful little things like that unless they're trying to impress a girl or get her in the sack."

"He's dating Summer, remember?"

"Whatever." She checked the clock on the wall. "It's almost three. Gavin should be here any minute now."

"You know when he's working? What did you do—take a peek at the master schedule?"

"No, I just asked him." Her eyes lit up as a lanky, surfer-looking guy strolled into The Purple Dog. "There he is."

"Oh, let's not be too obvious that you're into him or anything, shall we?" I pretended to be reading while I watched Gavin set his stuff under the counter and put on an apron. His straight blond hair fell into his eyes, which appeared to be blue. His tee shirt bore the logo of Casual Industries, a popular clothing line here in Seattle, and it stretched over his muscles as he moved. He was laughing at something one of his co-workers had said. "Not bad," I said once I finished my assessment.

"Yeah," Morgan agreed, her voice all dreamy. "I can't wait to get him naked."

"Isn't that moving a little fast?" Images from today's STD lecture flashed in front of my eyes, and I shuddered. As far as I knew, Morgan hadn't caught anything.

Yet.

She shrugged. "So maybe I'll try going slow for once, see where it leads."

"That sounds like a good plan." I turned back to the Faulkner novel I had to read for my second-period AP English class. "Maybe you'll be able to keep a guy longer than a week."

"Maybe." The way she said the word made it sound like she wasn't quite convinced it was such a good idea. "By the way, can we call your dad to help me with my philosophy assignment? I have so much to read, and it's so boring."

"Why did you take the class?"

"Pre-req." She held up the worn copy of Plato's *Symposium*, the neon orange "USED" sticker marring the image on the cover. "I'd love the quick rundown on this, and if he was willing to throw in some topics for a paper, I'd worship your dad forever."

"Don't even go there. You know how my dad is with his graduate assistants."

"Awesome book," a male voice with a distinct Southern Californian accent said behind me. I looked up to find Gavin standing with his hands on the back of my chair. "I wore my copy out from reading it over and over again."

He sounded like a stoner, but was obviously well acquainted with Plato. Must be a philosophy major.

"And what did you think of it?" Morgan asked sweetly.

"It's about love." Gavin let go of my chair and crossed his arms, sounding slightly more intelligent than before.

Morgan scribbled that down. "Like love between men and women?"

Gavin laughed. "Some, but there's some really interesting passages there about homosexuality."

Morgan sent me a panicked look that asked if she was chasing after the wrong type of guy.

I decided it was time to step in and save her. For once, the summers spent with my dad lecturing me about the great works of philosophy would come in handy. "Like Phaedrus's argument for gays in the military?"

"Or Aristophanes's tall tale about the origin of soul mates, babe." Gavin pulled a chair up to our table, staring at the words on my T-shirt peeking through my half-zipped hoodie. At least, I hoped that was what he was doing. Based on the time he spent staring at my chest, though, I could safely say he wasn't gay.

I pulled the zipper up on my hoodie, ignoring the little

warning bells going off in the back of my mind. "But then Socrates comes and basically calls them all idiots."

Gavin laughed harder this time. "Pretty much. Are you a philosophy major, too?"

Morgan was looking at us—or to be more precise, at Gavin looking at me—and frowning.

"My dad's a professor of philosophy." Time to divert his attention back to my best friend before I received a swift kick under the table for monopolizing the conversation. "Morgan is still undeclared, but she's leaning toward philosophy. Perhaps you can suggest some of your favorite works."

I immediately got the "what the hell are you doing" look from her.

"It's like asking me to pick a favorite wave on the North Shore of Oahu."

"Just a few suggestions, then, 'to fondle the interest in a potential lover of philosophy,' " I replied, quoting a line from Plato's *Symposium*.

He paused, and then tapped Morgan's book with a wider grin. "Ah, Socrates, nice."

And now we were back to the "shut the hell up around the guy I like" glare from Morgan. I squirmed in my seat, feeling a little bit too warm under the intensity of their heated attention. I got the distinct impression Gavin was flirting with me, and Morgan was getting pissed off. I longed to shed my hoodie, but I didn't want to flaunt my "Huge Tracts of Land" and make this situation even more awkward than it already was.

Gavin started rattling off some of the well-known classics: Aristotle. Augustine. Thomas Aquinas. Machiavelli. Descartes. Pascal. Hume. Locke. All stuff covered in a Philosophy 101 class.

When he finished, I said, "All classics. Perhaps you'd be willing to discuss some of them with Morgan as she reads them."

His gaze flickered over to her before turning back to me. "Okay."

Morgan's eyes widened. She finally saw where I was going with all this. "Yes, Gavin, I'd love to talk about philosophy with you any time."

His smile tightened. Not a good sign. "Sure, Morgan. Now, if you two ladies will excuse me, I gotta get back to work."

As soon as he was out of hearing range, my best friend gave me a small squeal. "That was brilliant, Alexis. I'd much rather have him as my philosophy tutor than your dad."

"Well, then, start reading so you have something to discuss with him."

She bent back over her book, reading Plato with far more enthusiasm now that she knew it would get her something outside of the classroom.

I tried to focus on my own homework, but I couldn't shake the uneasy feeling I got from Gavin. He seemed more interested in me than in my best friend, and that always spelled trouble.

"What does it take to get a letterman jacket? Athletic talent. Or, in the case of Benji Gapul, a $25,000 donation to the school's athletic program courtesy of Daddy."

The Eastline Spy
December, Freshman Year

Chapter 5

Thursday got off to a much better start. I was able to get a good night's sleep without having a screaming electronic doll waking me all night long. I had plenty of time to shower and add some de-frizzer to my hair. And I wasn't wearing any suggestive T-shirts (unless you considered the Batman logo suggestive).

Brett texted me to say he'd meet me at my locker for the doll handoff. I drove to school, my stomach doing little flip-flops of glee, anticipating that Brett would look as miserable as I felt yesterday.

No such luck.

If anything, the jerk looked better than normal.

Damn it.

He grinned and started unstrapping the carrier when he saw me. "Made it on time today, eh?"

"How can you be so cheerful after that thing kept

screaming all night?"

"I've got the diaper-bottle-burp drill down. Once you have it, you'll see it's easier with babies." He held out the carrier with the doll still strapped inside. "Should I help you put it on again?"

"So you can feel me up in the process?" He was so perfect, it was infuriating, so I had to find a flaw in him. In this case, it was turning his offer to help into a dick move.

"If that's an invitation…"

Sure, if you want to, that traitorous little voice in my head replied.

"It's not," I snapped, ignoring the rush of heat that flowed along the surface of my skin while I tried to navigate my arms through the confusing tangle of straps.

He raised both brows. "Are you always this stubborn?"

"I don't need a man to help me out with something as simple as this." Except somehow, I'd managed to put the carrier on upside down and was holding the doll by its head to keep it from falling out.

"May I please help you so we don't both end up with Fs because you dropped the kid?" He came closer, that annoying bemused grin still on his face, and took the doll out of the carrier. "Just unbuckle it here, turn it around, and secure everything before you try to put the baby in."

His finger brushed the area along my ribs when he pointed out where I should unbuckle it, and a delicious shiver raced up my spine. I hated my hormones sometimes, especially when they overruled my brain concerning Brett Pederson. It was screaming for me to run away before I made a fool of myself by drooling over him, but I ended up inching closer to him. I'd always thought his eyes were plain brown, but the sun streaming in from the skylight above revealed tiny flecks of green and gold in them.

And those eyes were fixed right on me.

"Yo, Pederson, you're playing a dangerous game getting that close to her without protective equipment on," Sanchez shouted from down the hall, ruining what had been a "moment."

As if I was capable of having a moment with Brett.

"I've got it under control," Brett shouted back before dropping his voice to add, "You're not going to hurt me, right?"

"Depends."

"On what?" He wasn't backing away, so neither would I.

"On how pissed off you're going to make me."

"And how would I piss you off?"

He was baiting me. I knew he was, and yet I played right along with him. "Your existence pisses me off."

"Is that all?" His grin widened.

The asshole was mocking me.

"Do I need to make you a list?" I shoved him back and adjusted the carrier, following his instructions.

"Maybe. How long would that list be?"

I snatched the doll back and tucked it away. "Not worth my time."

I'd barely made it ten feet before Richard fell into step beside me. "Okay, what is going on between you two, because that was some serious tension?"

"The only tension between us is the one in my arm that's keeping me from slapping that arrogant little smirk off his face."

Richard pretended to cover his mouth, mimicking a shocked expression. "Oh my God, you've progressed to violent thoughts. Do we need to schedule an intervention at the fro-yo place this afternoon so we get all that hostility out over a cup of mocha chocolate chip?"

"No, thank you." I liked my hostility right where it was. It was the only thing keeping me from admitting that yeah, maybe I was slightly attracted to Brett.

I glanced over my shoulder just in time to see Summer looping her arm through his. The message was as clear as day. He was hers, and I had no chance in hell of ending up with someone like him.

Not that I'd want to. It would mean I'd have to be nice to Sanchez and the rest of the team.

But that didn't keep me from thinking about how things might be different if we weren't in this tiny microcosm of hell called high school.

***

I stiffened the moment Brett slid into the chair next me, Richard's accusations still whirling around in my mind. *Go to that angry place. Go to that angry place.*

But he shifted ever so slightly, sending a current of his scent toward me. I breathed him in and crumbled. Who was I kidding? Brett was like one of those addictions that needed its own twelve step program. The first step was admitting you have a problem.

Hi, my name is Alexis Wyndham, and I have the hots for the quarterback.

I could just imagine a chorus full of girls from this high school answering back, "Hi, Alexis."

At least I wasn't alone with infatuation.

Because that's all it really could be, anyway. The Queen Bitch and the Football King had no business being together. It might trigger some space-time continuum implosion.

Mr. DePaul dimmed the lights and started another

PowerPoint presentation, his voice wry with an undercurrent of resentment. "I think this topic belongs in your Econ curriculum, but I was allowed to give you the safe sex lecture only if I agreed to give the following talk about the costs involved in raising a child. I suppose it's the school board's hope that once you see how expensive real kids are, you'll wait until you have a stable job before having any."

I only half listened as he droned on and on about things like diapers and saving for college. It was stuff my parents worried about, not me. Just one more reason to keep my legs crossed. If I don't give up my V card, I won't have to worry about having a real baby strapped to my chest and screaming at all hours of the night while deducting from my book budget.

The lecture was just coming to an end when Mr. DePaul went to his desk and clicked something. My computer pinged, announcing the arrival of a new email in my school account.

"If you check your inboxes, you'll find tonight's assignment," Mr. DePaul said in such a way, I almost expected him to roll his eyes. "Consider this just a taste of family budgeting."

I opened the attachment in the email and scanned the instructions. "Diapers? Formula?"

"Yeah, those things add up." Brett remained so nonchalant about it, I wondered if he'd even read the assignment until he added, "So, you want to meet up at Safeway after school and knock it out?"

"I'm actually done with school for the day."

"So am I." He slung his backpack over his shoulder and jerked his head toward the door. "Want to meet me there in fifteen minutes?"

Oh, crap. It was one thing to be seen with him at school. At least it was all under the confines of this class. But out of the classroom? And in a place where I'd be in danger of exposing my go-to stress eats by stocking up on Cheetos and mocha fudge ripple ice cream.

"Yoo-hoo? Lexi?" Brett asked, waving his hand in front of my face.

"Don't call me that." I slammed my laptop closed and stuffed it in my back. "I'll meet you there so we can get this over with as quickly as possible."

"See you there." He waved and walked to where Summer was waiting for him by the door.

Shit! How much of our conversation had she overheard? I just hoped she wouldn't insist on tagging along. If she did, I'd let Brett complete this assignment on his own. I had a daily bullshit limit, and he'd already reached it this morning.

"After sneaking into the school cafeteria yesterday and taking a peek in the fridge, I will be dining off campus from here on out. Please note the expiration dates on the food in the picture below."

The Eastline Spy
October, Sophomore Year

Chapter 6

The damn infant carrier got tangled in my seatbelt as I tried to get out of my car. And who else would be nearby to witness it than Brett? Laughter filled his dark eyes as he rushed to my side to rescue me like I was some damsel in distress. "Hold on a minute, Lexi. Let me help."

"How many times do I have to tell you to stop calling me that? And I don't need your help." I swatted at this hands while simultaneously tugging at the nylon belt wrapped around Junior. It was bad enough he insisted on calling by that name. I wasn't going to offer him another opportunity to feel me up, especially since my treacherous hormones got some sort of cheap thrill from it all.

He stepped back, and after thirty seconds of graceless fumbling, I managed to free myself and Junior without tipping him out of the carrier and earning us both an F. I looked back at him, lifting my chin in defiance as I straightened the plastic doll that was quickly becoming the bane of my existence. "See?"

"Good grief, you're stubborn." He shook his head and headed toward the sliding glass doors of the supermarket. Without pausing for a second, he cut a direct path for the baby aisle.

It was all foreign territory for me. I stared at the neat rows of glossy diaper packages and brightly colored baby food pouches, and my heart immediately started pounding in the center of my chest like a base drum. I licked my lips. "Um, what were supposed to do again for this assignment?"

"Calculate a budget for the cost of Junior's first year." He rubbed the doll's head like it was a pet dog. "This kiddo's going to be expensive."

"What do you mean?"

"Take diapers for example. He'll go through about twelve of those a day for the first couple of months, then maybe get down to about six to eight a day by his first birthday." Brett pulled out his phone and entered some numbers. "If we average it out the eight a day, he'll go through almost three thousand diapers during his first year."

I eyed the price tag next to a pack of Pampers, and my pulse quickened. "Diapers cost that much?"

Brett nodded and pointed down the aisle at the white plastic containers. "Wait until you see how much formula costs."

I checked the price of it and immediately felt queasy. "Note to self: Win the lottery before having a kid."

"Of course there are cheaper alternatives like cloth diapers and breast-feeding." His gaze zeroed in on the center of my chest.

"Hey, eyes up here, remember?"

"What?" he said in mock innocence. His grin told me once again, he enjoyed getting a rise out of me. "You obviously have the proper equipment."

"You know, why don't I finish this part of the assignment alone so you can have a quick romp with Summer under the bleachers before football practice?" I pulled out my phone and started snapping pictures of the price tags for diapers, formula, and baby food. I'd figure it all out when I got home. Just anything to get away from him.

"What do you have against Summer?"

"Long story." I picked up a jar of pureed green beans and wondered who would feed the icky green mush to their child.

"I have time to listen."

He was standing so close behind me, I could feel the heat radiating from his body along the nape of my neck. I refused to believe it was a flush from anger or embarrassment or the attraction I was so desperately trying to keep in check. No, it had to be from him invading my personal space.

And yet, I didn't want to push him away. At least, not right now. "It's ancient history."

"It's more than that based on the jabs you take at each other."

The thought of Summer making snide remarks about me stiffened my spine, and I spun around to find Brett mere inches away from me. I backed up, my back pressed against the cushiony packs of diapers. It would be so easy to tell him every dirty little secret about Summer, about how she'd once been my best friend and then stabbed me in the back. Perhaps it might even spare him from suffering the same fate once she decided there was someone else more worthy of her status. But would he even believe me? Or was he so ensnared by his girlfriend's wiles that he'd dismiss anything negative that I'd reveal to him.

"I don't know what she's told you, but she showed me who she really was back in junior high, and her actions helped shape me into the person I am now."

Brett arched a bow. "Is that so?"

"She's the one who inspired me to start my blog." Usually, just the mention of the Eastline Spy scared off any person who tried to confront me, but not Brett.

"Summer's the one who inspired to dig up dirt on everyone at school and post it for the world to see?"

"You make it sound like it's a bad thing."

"It is when you use it to intimidate people."

"I'm judicious with what I post." I tried to slide down toward the bottles, but Brett stiff-armed the shelves either side of me, trapping me against the Huggies. "Everyone has secrets. I only choose to expose what I consider to be wrong-doings, to bring justice to those who need to be knocked down a few pegs and to keep the administration from covering things up. Sometimes, the truth needs to be told for the good of the school, and I have no problem dishing it up."

"With an extra side of bitchiness." His brows drew together. "You use your blog to intimidate others, and yet you consider it an instrument of justice?"

I pointed to the Batman logo on the center of my shirt. "Just call me the Dark Knight."

The corner of his mouth quirked up into a wry smile, and he leaned in until his face was inches from mine. "And is there anything I have to be afraid of?"

His question bathed lips, and my spit dried up. Damn it, why did he have to be so good looking? I mean really good looking. Like he could be a model or something. That uneasy trickle of desire squirmed between my shoulder blades and dug its way into the pit of my stomach. My breath caught. If anyone needed to be afraid, it was me. It would be far too easy to fall under his spell.

I swallowed hard and found my voice again. "Not you, Teflon Boy."

He laughed and pushed off the shelves, his arms falling to his sides again. "You get to be Batman, and I'm just Teflon Boy?"

"Face it—I'm just cooler than you." I side-stepped away, thankful for the growing space between us. "Besides, you're the golden boy. Nothing sticks to you. For all I know, you could be shooting up steroids in the locker room and banging every cheerleader on the squad, and no one would know about it. They'll go to great lengths to hide your secrets."

That silenced his amusement. "And why do you think I have any secrets that need to be covered up?"

"Because you can't be as perfect as everyone thinks you are. There has to be something you're trying to hide."

He cocked his head to the side and stared at me. "You know what your problem is?"

"Enlighten me, Football Boy."

"You're always trying to find the bad in people."

"Because nine times out of ten, I'll find it."

He opened his mouth to counter my argument, but in the end, he just sighed and stuffed his hands in his pockets. "I guess if you look at people that way, you'll never be disappointed."

Or taken advantage of, which was exactly what Summer had done to me years ago. I had been the first stone she'd stomped on during her ascent to becoming the most popular girl in school, but I'd learned my lesson. And I wasn't going to reveal any vulnerability to Brett. "Are you suggesting there's a better way to keep the assholes out there in line?"

"Nope, but have you ever considered spotlighting a person who was doing something good for a change? Maybe it'll erase some of that negativity that surrounds you."

"Are you trying to tell me what to do with my blog?"

He shook his head. "Just making an assessment."

"You can stop trying to convince me to lay off your little circle of friends." I turned back to baby food. "Just help me calculate how many of these pouches I need for Junior."

"Two to three a day for six months." His phone buzzed, and he checked the message. "I've got to run, but could you please send me those pics of the price tags when you get a chance?"

"Are you sure you want to receive pictures from me?"

"You're welcome to send me any pictures you want."

His gaze fell back to my chest, and split second, I wondered if he was the one behind the camera in the girl's locker room. Of course, I dismissed it the moment I thought of it. He probably had dozens of girls sending him pictures of their cleavage. And who knew what Summer was sending him? No, Brett wasn't the type of guy so desperate to see naked women that he'd put a camera in the locker room to spy on them.

It still bothered me that I never found out who was behind the video. I'd love to call out that pervert to everyone in the school. But until I had a name, I would keep quiet about it to protect Taylor.

"You'll get baby food and diaper prices when I get home." I turned back to snapping shots of price tags, figuring he would be on his way.

I never expected him to sneak up behind me and whisper in my ear, "I think you're hiding something, too, you know."

I froze, paralyzed by the intimacy of the situation. Now,

he'd not only invaded my personal space. He was trying to burrow beneath my Queen B exterior. My voice shook ever so slightly as I asked, "Oh?"

"I don't think you're as cold-hearted as everyone thinks you are."

I refused to look at him for fear he'd see how dead on he was. My eyelids fluttered as I tried to pull myself together. I wouldn't let some jock destroy everything I'd spent the last three years building. I was hard. I was cruel. I didn't let people get to me. I was the Queen B. "You're wrong."

He laughed and backed away. His brown eyes danced with amusement as he crossed his heart. "Don't worry, Batman. Your secret is safe with me."

The phrase, "Piss off", sat poised on the tip of my tongue, and the balled up fists remained at my side as he disappeared around the end of the aisle, his attention now shifted to the text message he was typing out. As much as I wanted to prove to Brett that he was full of it, a doubt in the back of my mind held me back. Everyone except Richard and Morgan dismissed me as the biggest bitch in school without giving me a second look. But for some reason, Brett was spending an exorbitant amount of time trying to figure me out. He'd even switched places with someone to work with me.

And I had no idea why.

Some small part of me secretly wished it was because he liked me, but I knew better than to nurture that notion. Morgan's warning from the other day pealed in the back of my mind. He was probably trying to dig up something on me to give to his girlfriend. Instead of going gooey on the inside every time he got within a few inches of me, I needed to focus on making sure I didn't reveal anything Summer could use against me.

And that included secret crushes.

I'd already learned that lesson the hard way.

***

I was searching for something edible in the fridge that evening when I heard the garage door open. It was too early for Taylor to be back from cheerleading practice, and even then, she wouldn't come through the garage due to her lack of a driver's license. That only left one person.

"Hi, Mom," I said, looking up from the scant selection on the shelves. Of course, the one day I actually needed to buy food at the grocery store, I didn't. I'll blame Brett for distracting me. But it still didn't give me much hope for dinner. Did I want a PBJ sandwich again tonight, or did I want to try the freezer and hope there were enough veggies for a stir-fry? "No class tonight?"

My mom had been staying late after work for the last three weeks learning how to use a laser for facial resurfacing. Some plastic surgeon in town was teaching her, but my mom said she needed a certain number of hours of training before she could use it in her practice. Hence, why I'd barely seen her since school started.

"Nope, Pete was sick." Her high heels clicked across the tiled floor as she came up behind me. "Time for me to schedule another grocery delivery, huh?"

"Or you could just go to the grocery store like a normal mom."

Of course, there was nothing normal about my mom. A former beauty queen, she was elegant, intelligent, poised. More than once, I'd heard guys at school call her a MILF, which was disturbing. Of course, it didn't help that she looked more like an older sister than a mom thanks to her using her dermatologic knowledge on herself. I suspected she and her partner took turns injecting each other with Botox on their lunch breaks.

Taylor and my mom were cut from the same cloth, all about appearances.

I was more like my dad, valuing knowledge over beauty. Hence, why Mom and I always seemed to have a strained relationship, at best.

"You know how I hate going to the grocery store, honey. I keep running into my patients there, and they keep wanting to show me some skin growth in the produce section." She closed the fridge door. "Why don't we order pizza tonight?"

Part of me wanted to suggest she cook dinner for once, but I knew better. There was a reason why our kitchen still looked showroom new even though the appliances were five years old. "I'm cool with that, but you know Taylor will only eat a salad."

"Oh, that sounds like a better idea." She pulled her iPad out and started pressing buttons on the screen. "Do you want one, too?"

"No, thanks, Mom. I'm all about indulging in cheese, grease, and carbs." But when she handed the iPad to me to pick out my pizza toppings, I ended up loading up on the veggies.

That was when the Demon Doll decided to start screaming.

My normally graceful mom stumbled in her stilettos. "Holy shit, what is that?"

"Class project." I gave her back the iPad and began my checklist. Removing and replacing the diaper? Check, with still more screaming. Bottle in mouth? Check. Problem solved. I settled onto one of the barstools at the kitchen island and pretended to feed the doll.

"They've come a long way from the flour sack baby I had to tote around in school." Mom came closer, staring at it as though she expected it to turn into Chucky. "How did you get it to stop crying?"

"There's a sensor in its mouth that recognizes the bottle." I took it out to show, reviving the wails of displeasure from the doll. Peace returned as soon as I put the bottle back in the doll's mouth. "I'm getting graded on how well I take care of a doll that's meant to mimic a real baby."

"Definitely realistic." She returned to her iPad. "Is this the first day of the project?"

"It's the third." It didn't surprise me one bit that she slept through the screaming on Tuesday night. I suspected she'd taken an Ambien that night. "Brett and I are switching off every night, though."

"Who's Brett?"

"My partner for the project." No need to explain anything else, like the way I seemed to lose IQ points whenever I was around him.

"That's nice of him to help out with the baby, unlike your father."

I rolled my eyes and bit my tongue. I was used to the jabs she threw at Dad whenever she got a chance. What little I remembered of the divorce was messy. Mom had caught him fooling around with his graduate assistant. He claimed she'd driven him to it because she was too busy working all the time. In truth, I didn't care. My parents were better off split than they were together.

Thankfully, the front door slammed before I had to listen to any more. Taylor stopped at the edge of the kitchen. "What are you doing home this early, Mom?"

She finally looked up from her iPad. "Geez, you make it

sound like I'm never here."

"You aren't," I replied and began the burping part of the doll's cycle. Maybe Brett was right about this being a drill. It was almost becoming second nature now. Perhaps there was some minute shred of a maternal gene in me.

Taylor dumped her cheerleading bags on the floor and sat on the barstool next to me. "It's just strange having you here at dinner time, that's all."

"Sounds like we're overdue for a family dinner, then." She handed Taylor the tablet. "Which salad do you want?"

"She always gets the Greek salad, dressing on the side, extra kalamata olives," I answered. I'd ordered from this restaurant enough times to have it memorized.

Taylor nodded. "Yep, my usual."

Mom looked at her as though she was a stranger before entering the order. A few clicks later, and she put the tablet down on the counter. "Time to get comfy."

Once she left the kitchen, Taylor pounced on the iPad and started typing in a web address. "I don't know what you did, but those videos are down. See?"

She held up the tablet so I could see the site, which said the videos had been removed by the user.

"Glad to know the secrets of your cleavage are safe—at least, until some guy tries to get to second base."

She smacked me with the iPad. "You are so crude sometimes."

"You're the one insisting on wearing the inserts."

She gave me an exaggerated huff. "And here I was, trying to thank you for getting them taken down."

"Wait, what was that?" I held my hand up to my ear. "You're thanking me?"

"Whatever. But for once, I'm glad the biggest bitch in

60

Eastline is my sister." A hint of sincerity laced her voice, and she gave me a hug.

My throat started to swell, blocking off any words that could ruin this rare display of affection from Taylor.

She rolled off the barstool. "I'm going to change and get started on my homework. Let me know when the food gets here."

And just like that, I was back to being alone in our barely used kitchen.

"One step forward, then two steps back. The school administration announced today that there would be zero tolerance for sexual harassment of any kind. Then they unveiled next year's cheerleading uniform, which is an inch shorter than this year's. Way to go, Eastline!"

The Eastline Spy
June, Sophomore Year

Chapter 7

Friday morning was looking halfway decent. I actually managed to get some sleep between crying fits. Maybe because I followed Brett's advice about the diaper-bottle-burp drill. My hair was tamed, my teeth were brushed, and my Hello Kitty tee was giving the world a middle finger.

Even better was the fact Brett stood waiting at my locker with another steaming cup of coffee. He eyed my shirt. "Well, that's saying something."

I grinned. "Ready for Junior?"

We swapped the doll and the coffee, but as he was putting on the carrier, he cleared his throat and said, "Um, can I ask a favor of you, Alexis?"

"What?" It was bad enough that it was a Friday during football season. On game days, the football players paraded around campus in their jerseys like they were kings, and the cheerleaders pranced around in short skirts that left little to the imagination. Hence why I chose the "Up Yours" T-shirt this morning.

"I need you to watch Junior tonight."

"You've got to be frigging kidding me."

I started to turn away, but he caught my shoulder and guided me back with a gentleness I wouldn't have expected from a testosterone-laced jock. "Just for the game tonight. I couldn't get Sarah to babysit, and I don't want to leave the doll in the locker room."

"It's my night off from the kid."

"Please," he said, turning those warm chocolate-colored eyes on me as though they might melt my resistance.

"I have plans," I lied.

"No, you don't. I already asked Taylor."

Remind me to pay her back for that later.

"Since when is she the expert on my social calendar?"

"Ah, come on, Lexi, it's just for a few hours. Pick up the doll before kickoff, let me play the game, and I'll take him back as soon as it's over. It's better than the alternative." He nodded down the hallway, where Sanchez and another football player were pretending to drop an alley-oop using some freshman's homework.

Sanchez then crashed into the lockers and laughed it off like he meant to do it.

Idiot.

Brett gave me the look that probably made every girl in Eastline sigh, but when it didn't work on me, he added, "Please."

I closed my eyes, knowing I was going to regret the next few words that came from my mouth. "Fine, I'll take him off your hands for a few hours."

"Thank you, Lexi. Gotta run and make sure my star wide receiver doesn't land on the DL before the game starts." Brett took off down the hall and pulled Sanchez aside, hopefully telling him what dumbass he was being.

Less than thirty seconds later, I was stopped by a teacher and informed my shirt was in violation of the dress code.

I returned to my locker for my hoodie and zipped it just high enough to cover the offensive paw and appease the dress code enforcer. Then, as soon as she was out of sight, I lowered the zipper.

I hate high school.

***

It wasn't until fourth period that I realized what I'd agreed to do. It started when Brett sat down next to me and said, "The game starts at seven, but if you could come by at six to take Junior, that'd be perfect."

"You mean I have to come back here to get him? During a football game?" My pulse cranked up a notch. I'd managed to make it through three years of high school without attending a single football game, and he was trying to break my perfect record.

"Didn't you hear what I said this morning?"

"No, I was too busy being pissed off that you were dumping the doll on me."

He rolled his eyes. "Has anyone ever told you that you catch more flies with honey than vinegar?"

I leaned closer to him, adding a threatening edge to my voice. "Are you suggesting I should try being nice?"

"Would it kill you?"

"It is much safer to be feared than loved," I replied.

"This is not Renaissance Florence, and you are not Lorenzo de' Medici," he replied, totally catching my reference from Machiavelli's *The Prince.*

I took in a deep breath, preparing to launch on a tirade that would finally shut him up, but paused when he didn't back away. Instead, he came closer, and the air around us crackled with something. Maybe it was anger. Maybe it was sexual attraction. I don't know, and I didn't care at that moment. I'd discovered my Achilles heel.

It was hard to think straight when I was around him.

"If you want to be happy, practice compassion."

The quote rendered me speechless. Where the hell did that come from? It was the exact opposite of what I'd thrown at him, so simple and yet so deep coming from a dumb jock.

"That's from the Dalai Lama, by the way," he said with a wink. "Good advice, if you ask me."

"I didn't."

"Well, maybe you'd be less bitchy if you followed it once in a while."

"And what if I like being bitchy?"

He looked at me as though I were the one who'd sustained one too many hits to the head. "Seriously?"

"Seriously."

"I think you're full of shit."

Mr. DePaul ended the conversation before I could give my rebuttal. I stewed over my conversation with Brett instead of paying attention to what our teacher was talking about. Something about family planning. I didn't give a damn. I was more focused on trying to prove to Brett that I was perfectly happy with being the Queen B of Eastline.

Except, if I was really being honest with myself, I sometimes felt a stab of envy when I looked at the way people fawned over the popular kids. As stuck-up and superficial as Summer Hoyt was, she still had people who wanted to be like her. People like my airhead sister. Brett was Mr. Superstar Starting Quarterback and Student Body President, a leader both on and off the field everyone admired.

I didn't have anyone wanting to be my protégé. The only people in the school who didn't flee from me when I was in one of my Queen B moods were Morgan and Richard.

And now Brett.

Shit, I was getting soft in my old age.

I made a mental note to dig up some dirt on a few popular kids for my blog before I left campus today, if only to make up for the ground I was losing with Brett.

The bell rang before I knew it, and Brett whispered in my ear, "So I'll see you outside the locker room at six?"

I fought hard to maintain my angry glare. "Maybe."

"Aw, come on, Lexi, it's just for a few hours."

"Stop calling me that. Do you have some sort of death wish?"

His eyes flickered up and down, from my face to my shirt and back again. A slow easy smile appeared on his face. "Maybe."

He slipped out of the classroom before I could think of a good comeback.

Damn him.

The only upside to the day was that was time for my weekly blog post to go live. Since the offensive videos had come down, I felt it was now safe to go public with what was obviously a violation of privacy but still keep it vague enough to protect my sister. I took a moment to re-read what I'd written last night.

It appears nothing is sacred here on campus. Yes, I've been known to use a camera here and there to expose wrong-doings, but I've never stooped to the audacity someone in this school recently has.

Earlier this week, it came to my attention that someone had planted a camera on campus and was recording certain members of the student body and streaming them on YouTube. Due to the sensitive nature of these videos, I took it upon myself to remove the camera and dispose of it. Thankfully, my message to the voyeur got through because the videos have since been taken down by the user.

But it brings up a set of bigger issues.

> *1.   That this happened in our school without the administration being aware of it.*
>
> *2.   That someone felt it was perfectly acceptable to violate the privacy of our female students in such a way.*
>
> *3.   That the identity of that pervert was never discovered.*

So take this as a warning, whoever was behind the hidden camera. If you dare try something like this again, I will personally make it my mission to hunt you down and expose you to everyone in the school.

I hit *Post* and packed away my laptop, relieved I was able to let that asshole know I wouldn't show any mercy next time.

Now, I needed to figure out if I was willing to show the same hard-nosed stance with Brett.

"Hooray to our football team for winning the state championship! And an even bigger congrats goes to the senior star running back, Jamal Washington, for getting a 4.0 this semester, even in the first period class that he only attended once since school started."

The Eastline Spy
December, Freshman Year

Chapter 8

I caved.

At six o'clock, I met Brett at the locker room door.

My breath hitched when I saw him. He was shirtless and looked so good it bordered on criminal. His brown skin stretched over well-defined muscles that would have a sculptor in ecstasy. I was counting my way down his six-pack when I came to the waist of his low-slung, tight-fitting pants. What I wouldn't give to let my gaze keep traveling south.

Instead, I got a view of the black infant carrier hanging from his outstretched hand and the mechanical doll that was becoming the bane of my existence.

"Thank you again, Lexi."

I didn't dare open my mouth to correct him. I might start drooling like an idiot.

"I'll meet you back here after the game." He ducked back

into the room filled with other half-naked boys, some of whom I wished had kept their shirts on.

I wandered around campus for the next half hour before ending up back at my car, trying to decide if it was worth hanging around to watch the game versus going out to a coffee shop with Junior. I hated to admit that Taylor was right—I didn't have any plans for tonight. Morgan had invited me to hang out at The Purple Dog, but when she heard I had baby duty, she told me to stay home. I had no idea what Richard did on Friday nights. I felt alone—really, really alone—and for a moment, I wished I had more friends.

The sounds of conversations punctuated by laughter drifted over from the football field, mingling with the steady *rat-a-tat-tat* of the drum line. People walked past me with smiles on their faces in anticipation of the first home game of the season. My curiosity got the better of me, so I crept toward the stands, paid my admission, and stuck to the shadows in the hopes no one would recognize me.

"Oh my God, is that you, Alexis?" Richard asked from behind me.

I yelped and spun around. "Don't sneak up on me like that."

"Sorry, but I needed to make sure hell hadn't frozen over." He gave me a fake shiver. "I thought you said you wouldn't be caught dead at a football game."

"Yeah, but unfortunately, I ended up with Brett Pederson's baby," I replied, gesturing to the doll strapped to my chest.

"You have no idea how many girls would love to be in your position. Hell, I'd love to have his baby except for, you know, the actual childcare part." He hooked his arm around mine. "Let's go find a seat, shall we?"

"You're here for the game?" Somehow, football didn't

seem like an event that would attract Richard.

"I never miss them."

I stared at him like he'd grown another head. "But it's like the most caveman-macho thing out there."

"No, it's not." He pointed to the players who were warming up on the field. "Think about it. A bunch of guys wearing tight pants, slapping each other on the ass, tackling each other to the ground. The only thing that's more gay is wrestling."

He led us to an empty spot on the bleachers right in front of the bench and led us there. "I think this has a nice view, don't you think?" he asked as he sat down.

I looked to where he was pointing and discovered a nice view of Brett's ass. "Possibly."

"Are you sure you're straight? I mean, if I had a chance to work side by side with Brett, I'd be all over that boy."

"He's the most infuriating guy I've ever met."

"Denial." He crossed his legs and rested his hands on his knee. "We need to have that therapy session over fro-yo and figure out a way to get you some action."

"I don't need any action with him."

"Bullshit. Besides, this isn't about needs. It's about wants, and I saw that little exchange between you two yesterday." He gave me an evil grin. "You totally want him."

"What I really want is to be done with high school and off to college."

"And I want to be in the middle of a Johnny Weir and Adam Lambert sandwich, but I still have to make do with what I have in the meantime. Like this." He held out his hands toward the field. "So, I'm making the best of it and rating all the players on my Gay-o-Meter."

Laughter forced its way up my throat and spilled over. I

could just imagine Richard writing little comments along the roster about who he thought was hiding in the closet.

"But if you had a choice, would you rather be here or at a club on Capitol Hill?" I asked once I stopped laughing.

"Why not both in one night?" He pulled out his wallet and showed me the shiny new fake ID. "Morgan hooked me up."

"You look more twelve than twenty-one."

"Fuck you." He put away his wallet. "Actually, I take that back. I don't want to fuck you. Sorry, but you don't have a penis."

"No apologies necessary."

I scanned the stadium, taking in the atmosphere. The scents of kettle corn and hot dogs wafted over from the concession stand. The megawatt lights chased away the darkness and created a world of daytime brightness. The chants of the cheerleaders echoed through the crowd, growing louder by the second.

Beside me, Richard chanted right along with them, mocking their pompom shaking movements. At the end, he stood up and wiggled his ass like the dance team girls did in their tiny skirts below, earning matching frowns from Summer and Taylor. "See, I told you I'd make an awesome cheerleader," he said as he sat back down.

"I'm not arguing with you. I think it sucks that they wouldn't let you on the squad."

"They just aren't ready to handle all this." He gestured to his thin-framed body that made him look younger than his sixteen years.

"More like they were all worried you'd flirt with the players and steal their boyfriends."

"I like how you think." He laid his head on my shoulder. "One of the many reasons I love you, Alexis."

My heart hiccupped at that moment. I had to admit, it felt good to be loved. My thoughts turned to my conversation with Brett earlier today. "Richard, do you think I should try to be nicer?"

His eyes widened. "Have you been drinking?"

"No, but it's sometimes exhausting to be the Queen B, 24/7."

"I know it's always exhausting to re-establish your place at the beginning of the year, but don't go soft on me, please. If you do, then I lose the protection I've gained from being your friend."

I quirked a smile. "So is that the reason you're my friend? Because I offer you protection?"

"Damn straight, girlfriend. No one's going to bully me as long you're the Queen Bitch of Eastline. Of course, I'm dreading next year after you graduate and leave me here on my own."

"You'll be fine. And if you're still worried, I'll start prepping you to become the next Queen B."

"I don't know about that—it all depends on what the tiara looks like."

I bumped his shoulder with my own, laughing again and not caring who saw me. During the school day, I had to keep my game face on to rule as the Queen B. But now it was Friday night, and I was glad to have a friend I could joke around with, even if it meant letting others see I wasn't a total bitch to everyone.

"Besides," Richard continued, "I'm not sure I have enough bitchiness in me."

"You're as bitchy as the best of us."

"Aw, that's so sweet."

It was time for kickoff. As soon as the ball flew into the

air, I was lost. I had no idea what the game was about or if I should cheer or boo the refs. Thankfully, Richard knew more than enough to explain the basics to me.

One thing was very clear, however. Brett was a god on the football field. He walked onto it like he owned it. All the players gathered around him, turning to him for guidance. And when he had the ball in his hands, things happened that electrified the crowd. Sometimes he chose to keep it for himself and run. Other times, he'd launch the ball down the field with such precision, it left me speechless.

It was after one of those plays that Richard turned to me and said, "Now you know why he's one of the top high school players on the West Coast."

"He's better than the other quarterback—I'm not going to argue with you there—but one of the top players? Really?"

"He already has eight colleges begging for him to sign with them."

"Wow." But I could see why. He made it look so easy, so effortless as he shot the football in a tight spiral toward Sanchez. All the wide receiver had to do was hold his hands out, and the ball fell into them.

The perfect pass.

I was up on my feet, jumping and shouting with the rest of the crowd as Sanchez scampered into the end zone for a touchdown.

Something rolled in my stomach when I realized what I was doing. I'd drunk the Kool-Aid and joined the cult.

I sat back down and crossed my arms, pressing the doll into my cleavage. "Does he have any flaws?"

"None that I can see," Richard said in a dreamy voice, "except for the fact he seems to have something for you and not me."

"You mean because he's straight?"

"No, I mean because he's staring right at you."

I followed Richard's finger and found Brett standing on the sidelines just as he described. Our eyes met, and he winked at me before joining his teammates in high-fives.

My stomach rolled again for an entirely different reason.

Richard came closer and said just loud enough for me to hear, "Are you sure there's nothing between you two?"

"Absolutely nothing." I watched as Summer broke away from the other cheerleaders to plant a kiss on Brett's cheek. "How can there be when he's with her?"

"Yeah, bummer. Maybe he's not that perfect after all."

The game ended with Eastline completely demolishing their opponent. Richard mentioned something to me that Brett had broken some kind of passing record, which I assumed would only increase his attractiveness to the schools that would give him a free ride for his throwing arm. I had to admit that I'd enjoyed the experience, maybe enough to come back as long as I had Richard beside me with his colorful commentary.

We filed out of the stadium with the crowd and their infectious energy.

"So, are you taking Morgan's gift and hitting the clubs after this?" I asked.

Richard rolled his eyes. "I wish. My grandmother is in town, and I have to play straight for a few more days if I want her to give me a car."

"What?" I pulled him aside, wondering if I heard him correctly.

"My grandmother is old school from China. She doesn't get the fact that I'm gay, and frankly, if I told her, she might keel over and die, so I'm pretending to be straight when I'm around her until I get my car. Once I have it, then I'm free to go where I want and I can send her pictures of me kissing all the hot guys on Capitol Hill."

"And I thought I was evil."

"We all play games to get what we want, Alexis—you included—so don't judge me."

"I don't pretend to be something I'm not."

"Right, you just keep telling yourself that, but you and I both know you're lying." He pointed two fingers at his eyes and then at me. "I've been watching you, and I know someone's getting you all hot and bothered, but you're too proud to admit it because you think he's beneath you."

"Are you sure you aren't suffering from some temporary delusions brought on by too much pompom shaking?"

He gave me a middle finger. "Any time you want that therapy session, let me know."

"Thank you, Dr. Phil," I said as he walked away.

It took about fifteen minutes for the crowds to thin enough to let me get close to the locker room. I leaned against the wall, listening to the players celebrate inside and becoming thoroughly disgusted by all their smack talk. It made me wish I'd packed along something intelligent to read.

The door finally opened with a blast of Axe-scented steam, and the football team filed out. Of course, Brett was one of the last ones to leave. I held out the carrier for him. "Now that the game's over, here you go."

His eyes shifted from side to side, and a tight smile formed on his lips. "Um, yeah, about that..." He pulled me aside so we wouldn't trip up the other players.

My jaw clenched, followed by a flare of anger that sent flames dancing in front of my eyes. I shook his hands off my shoulders. "Don't you dare even suggest it."

"Please. Alexis, just until morning—"

Summer cut him off by drawling out his name from the exit of the girls' locker room. "Don't keep me waiting too long."

"Oh my God." I delivered each word like the punches my carefully restrained fists wanted to deliver. Instead, I had to rely on words because there was a good chance the entire team would jump me if I dared to injure their star quarterback. "You're dumping the doll on me for another night so you can go fuck your girlfriend?"

"She's not my girlfriend."

"Fuck buddy, then."

He opened his mouth, but nothing came out. A few blinks later, he asked, "Do you kiss your mother with that mouth?"

"Don't get all prudish on me. I know damn well you're a complete asshole who's just out to score off the field."

"And you're so indignant and self-righteous, you won't even let me get a word in edgewise."

Now it was my turn to be stunned silent and left blinking like an idiot. He'd pulled out words I didn't think were in a jock's vocabulary. He'd even used them correctly.

"What I was trying to say is that if you agree to watch Junior tonight, you can drop him off at my house bright and early tomorrow morning, and I'll take him all weekend. That way, you're free to do whatever it is you do on weekends without having to endanger our project."

"I don't know where you live."

"I'll text my address to you in a few minutes." He turned around to say something to Sanchez, who slapped him on the back and urged him to "dump the bitch and get going."

I crossed my arms, the doll dangling from the carrier in my hand. "We are not amused."

"A thousand apologies, Your Majesty," Brett said with a mocking bow. "So, will you please keep Junior overnight?"

"I can drop it off bright and early?"

"Absolutely."

"And you won't be too hungover to take care of Junior?"

"Not likely," he said with a cocky grin.

"And I won't run into Summer doing the walk of shame?"

He had the decency to choke on a laugh. "Not a chance."

That made me feel a little better. "If I don't get a text from you in ten minutes, I'll start calling and interrupting any action you were hoping of getting."

This time, he didn't try to cover up his chuckle. He pulled out his phone. "I'm sending it to you right now."

I heaved an exaggerated sigh. Another night of interrupted sleep, but it would be nice to be doll-free all weekend. "Fine. But I'll be there at eight a.m. on the dot."

"I'll be up and ready. And please wear something G-rated—I don't want to have to explain your T-shirt to my little sisters." His thumbs flew over the surface of his phone. A few seconds later, my phone beeped. "Now you have my address. Are we good?"

Before I could answer, Summer appeared and tugged on Brett's arm. "Come on. I don't want to be late."

All I could think about as they walked away was that I hoped he had enough good sense to wear a condom.

"Dear Ms. Carpenter, I know you desperately want to be elected Teacher of the Year by the student body, but supplying alcohol to students and partying with them on the weekend is not the way to do it."

The Eastline Spy
March, Sophomore Year

Chapter 9

Eight a.m. came and went because I decided to sleep in on Saturday. It was a little past nine before I finally looked up Brett's address.

He lived in my neighborhood, just two streets away from me.

How did I not know that?

I got dressed, remembering his request to keep the outfit G-rated and settling for a pair of jeans and a button-down shirt. Since he was so close, I decided it would be better to walk than drive. The last thing I wanted was for someone to see my car parked in front of his house. Just drop the doll off, and I was done.

Except he didn't answer the door. A young girl who looked a lot like him did.

"Is Brett here?" I asked, fully expecting to find out he was still in bed, or worse, had bailed on me.

"Yeah, he's in the den with the twins." The girl motioned for me to come inside. "I'm Sarah, his sister. You must be Alexis."

"I am." I stepped through the door and entered a home very unlike my own.

Like the kitchen, the rest of my house was in pretty much showroom condition, with the exception of Taylor's room. Mom had a maid service come in twice a week to clean, and the three of us all had such busy schedules that we were hardly ever in the house. Everything inside was hard and modern, pristine and cold.

Brett's house, on the other hand, had a definite lived-in appearance. A dozen pairs of shoes in various sizes and kinds lined the entryway. The furniture looked rumpled and comfy. Toys littered the next room. And a delicious aroma came from what looked to be a well-used kitchen.

But nothing prepared me for the sight that greeted me when I walked into the den. Brett was on his hands and knees, whinnying like a horse while two identical little girls giggled on top of his back.

I pulled out my phone and snapped a picture of the scene. I'd finally gotten some dirt on Brett Pederson.

An "oh shit" look crossed his face when he realized what I'd done. He sat up slowly, letting his little sisters slide off his back, and came toward me with caution guarding his movements. "Hi, Lexi."

"Having fun?" I quipped.

His spine straightened, and his normal air of confidence returned. "Um, yeah, actually, I am."

Okay, I had to give him props for admitting he enjoyed playing with his sisters.

One of the twins tugged on his arm. "Come back, horsey."

"Please!" the other chimed in, grabbing the other arm and pulling him back toward the castle play set. "We need you to finish playing Maximus."

Sarah stepped in and took the twins by the hands. "Brett has company. I'll play horsey for a little bit."

The little girls erupted in cheers and scampered back to their game.

"I told you my sister was good with kids," Brett said, the smudge of finger paint along his cheek only adding to my amusement. "Why don't we come this way?"

He pulled me into the hallway leading to the kitchen. "By the way, great blog post yesterday. Thank you for getting those videos taken down. They were stressing Summer out."

I bit back a retort. Of course he'd be thanking me for keeping his girlfriend's fake breasts from being displayed all over the internet. In helping my sister, I'd inadvertently helped my nemesis, too. But it was a small price to pay to keep Taylor safe.

I checked him over. No red eyes. No bags under them. No self-satisfied smirk. Only a really gnarly bruise peeking out from under the sleeve of his T-shirt, which I attributed to the game. "You're looking better than I expected."

"This is nothing." He rubbed the bruise on his arm. "You should've seen how banged up I was after playing Sky Lake last year."

If this was nothing, then I could only imagine what the players at the rival high school did to him. I wanted to ask him why he subjected his body to this weekly battering, but instead, we lapsed into an awkward silence I decided to break by offering the doll.

He didn't grab it right away. "Want to stay for breakfast?"

My stomach chose that moment to growl, and the mouthwatering aromas from the kitchen called to me. But my brain urged caution. "I should be going before someone catches me here."

"Why?" He took a step toward me, his grin daring me to answer him even though he obviously knew why.

I backed away, hitting the wall. Trapped. "Because I don't want people getting the wrong idea about us."

He kept closing in on me, propping his arm up against the wall. My pulse quickened, and my mouth grew dry. Usually, I was the one in power. Usually, I was the intimidator. Usually, I could keep my shit together around the popular kids and have a few quick verbal jabs at the ready for situations like this.

But nothing was usual about Brett.

He lowered his head, his lips inches from mine. Something inside my stomach bounced up and down like a hyper child on a trampoline. My breath caught.

But instead of kissing me like I thought he would, he moved his head to the side and dropped his voice into a whisper meant just for my ears. "Scared people will think we're fuck buddies?"

I couldn't stop my lips from curling up into a smile that matched his. "Do you kiss your mother with that mouth?"

He pushed back off the wall and strolled into the kitchen, taking the frying pan from his mother's hand and kissing her on the cheek. "I'll take over the pancakes, Mum."

"You're such a darling, Brett," she replied, a thick British accent adding a musical element to her words.

If she only knew what he'd said moments before.

"Oh, and I invited Lexi to breakfast."

"Welcome." She moved to the sink and began washing off fruit. I hadn't expected her to be Indian, but now I saw where Brett got his dark coloring and insanely thick eyelashes from.

The twins raced past me, jostling the doll that was still in the carrier in my hands. "Flip them, flip them," their little voices chimed.

Brett lifted the pan off the burner, shook it a couple of times, and flipped the pancake in the air, catching it back in the pan with well-practiced ease. The twins cheered, followed by cries for him to do it again.

He caught my eye, silently asking if I was impressed.

Coming from a household where punching the microwave's buttons was the extent of any cooking demonstrations I'd seen, I had to concede that yes, I was impressed.

"So, are you going to stay for breakfast?" he asked as he slid the cooked pancake onto a plate and buttered the pan for the next one.

"Does it taste as good as it smells?"

"Better. I'll even add blueberries to yours."

"Okay, you talked me into staying." I wasn't going to turn down a home-cooked meal, especially when it included entertainment.

But as soon as I sat down, one of the twins flopped into my lap with a blue ribbon. "I'm Rapunzel, and I need you to braid my hair."

Brett remained focused on breakfast, but his lips twitched. He must have enjoyed watching someone else boss me around for a change.

Sarah rushed over to intervene. "I can do that, Bitsy."

How she could tell the twins apart was beyond me, but I wasn't going to back down from a challenge, especially in front of Brett. I handed Sarah the doll instead. "I can braid her hair, if you don't mind making sure the doll is someplace safe."

Heaven only knew what those twins would do to it if they

got their paint-covered hands on it. It would make Brett's war paint look tame.

"I need you to braid it so I don't trip over it," Bitsy said, pretending hair was as long as the fairy tale character's.

"And when you're done with her, it's my turn," the other one demanded.

Brett shook with laughter at the stove.

I'd show him. "How about I braid the ribbon into your hair?"

That got met with a chorus of "ooohs," so I got to work. I may not be a fashionista who spent hours every morning perfecting my appearance, but I could braid hair. And thanks to Taylor making similar demands and a mom who was always too busy to do it, I'd gotten pretty good at it when we were younger. For a split second, I grew nostalgic for the time when my sister and I were still friends, when she looked up to me as her big sister instead of trying to deny that we were even related.

Bitsy's curls were a little challenging at first, but once I got them sorted out, I was able to weave the ribbon into her hair as I braided it, using the ends to tie it off when I was finished.

"My turn," the other twin said, shoving her sister out of my lap and crawling into the recently vacated spot. "I want you to do the same thing, but with a pink ribbon."

At least with the different-colored ribbons, I stood a chance of telling them apart. "And what's your name?"

"Evie." Unlike her sister, she sat very quietly like a prim and proper princess while I braided her hair.

I took the moment to lose myself in the mindless activity. It had been so long since I'd sat down with my own sister like this, I'd almost forgotten what it felt like to be a big sister and have fun. Now, I was constantly up against Taylor's "I'm a cheerleader" attitude and mediating the increasing arguments between her and Mom.

I was done with Evie's hair sooner than I wanted. Now that both little girls had their hair braided, they ran off into the den holding each other's hands and giggling.

Brett came to the table with two plates of pancakes. He set them down on the table and offered to help me up from my chair. "You're going to have to teach me how to do that."

Somehow, I wasn't surprised to learn Brett wanted to know how to braid hair. Maybe everyone was right—maybe he was perfect. I took his hand, and my skin tingled where his touched mine. An odd warmth filled my chest. My gaze was locked with his, and before I realized what I was doing, I was nodding like a mindless twit.

Damn, he was good. No wonder half of Eastline was in love with him.

Brett's mom came to the table carrying more plates piled high with pancakes. "Breakfast, everyone."

Brett led me to the bench against the wall and slid into the space next to me. I could feel the warmth from his thigh radiating through his jeans into my own. The rest of his family gathered around the table in chairs.

Brett's dad was the last person to come into the kitchen. If Brett got his coloring from his mom, he got his height and build from his dad. Mr. Pederson was easily six-two with broad shoulders, piercing blue eyes, and pale blond hair. He looked like a Nordic model, which further piqued my curiosity about Brett's family.

He stopped and studied me. "Who's that?"

"Brett's friend, Lexi," his mother replied as though Brett had friends over all the time.

Breakfast started with the usual passing of the syrup, but

once everyone had their pancakes prepped the way they liked them, everyone started eating.

Except me. The concept of a family gathered around a table for a meal was so foreign that I didn't know what to do.

Brett nudged me with his elbow, a large section already missing from his short stack. "I thought you were hungry."

"I am." I lifted the pancakes and peered between the layers. Steaming juice poured out from the plump blueberries and practically begged me to take a bite. "Just trying to make sure you haven't pranked me by putting hot sauce between them."

Sarah snickered from across the table. "I'll have to remember that."

"They're perfectly safe. I'll even sample them to prove it." He reached his fork toward my plate, but I blocked him.

"Hey, leave me something to eat." But it was now or never. I cut a small wedge out of my stack, put it in my mouth, and then lost every shred of self-control. They were awesome. I closed my eye and let the flavors sink into my taste buds. A soft moan broke free before I could stop it.

"Told you they were good," Brett murmured in my ear.

My body startled, sending the bite I had into the back of my throat and choking me. Oh, that was lovely. Here I was, not wanting people to know I was over at Brett's house, and I was going to choke to death at his breakfast table. A hand connected to my back, forcing the air from my lungs in a disgusting hack. Several coughs later, I was finally able to clear it. My cheeks burned once I finally was able to breathe again.

"You okay, Lexi?" Brett asked, genuine concern filling his dark eyes.

I nodded, not trusting what would come out of my mouth after a near-death experience. I reached for the glass of orange juice in front of me. Half a glass later, I was finally recovering from my embarrassment. "Fine."

He looked me over once more before returning to his meal. "So, whatcha planning on doing today?"

"Probably start filling out college applications," I replied. I really hadn't made any plans, but I knew those needed to be done soon.

"What schools are you looking at?" Brett's dad asked.

"Harvard, Yale, NYU, Duke—mostly stuff on the East Coast." I paused to take another bite, chewing it well and swallowing before I continued. "I was able to visit some of them over the summer with my dad, and I liked the feel of them. What about you, Brett?"

His dad answered for him. "Brett's waiting to see which schools offer him a football scholarship before deciding where he wants to go—isn't that right?"

I caught the slight frown from his mom and the grim smile from Brett as he answered, "Yeah, but it's still all up in the air. I mean, I don't have to decide anything yet, and I'm still waiting to see what all my options are."

Yep, this was definitely a tense issue in this family. I wondered if I should step in and change the subject, but his dad kept pushing it.

"Smart idea. Look how many calls you got this morning after last night's game."

Calls? This intrigued me. "I heard you broke some kind of record last night," I said.

"He broke the state's passing record for a single game," his father boasted, his chest puffed as though he'd been the one who broke the record and not his son.

"Erik, please," Brett's mom intervened, "this is not an appropriate conversation to have in front of our guest."

"You act like it's something to be ashamed of."

Brett's grip tightened on his fork, his knuckles blanching, but he said nothing. Suddenly, his life didn't seem so perfect. He was real, not some golden boy football god everyone revered. He had some serious issues going on beneath his perfect façade, and some hidden part of me finally felt a connection to him.

Which of course scared the shit out of me. I didn't want to care about Brett Pederson.

"No, I'm very proud of our son," his mother countered, her voice calm and smooth, "but football will not be his life. He is going to college for an education that will serve him for years to come, not to have a dozen men knock him to the ground every weekend."

For a second, I thought I saw Brett relax, but as soon as his dad spoke, the tension returned.

"And all I'm saying is that he has a talent that will get him into some of the best schools in the country for free, or did you not catch that phone call from the head coach of your alma mater this morning?"

If Brett was a pressure cooker, I sensed he was reaching the explosion point about now. I'd seen it too many times between my mom and my sis, and I reflexively reached over to calm him just as he shouted, "Dad!"

Brett stiffened, sucking in a breath as he looked down to where my hand rested on his arm.

Shit! I'd just crossed the line. And whether it was good or bad, it didn't matter. I'd intervened and given him proof that I wanted to help, that I actually cared.

I yanked my hand back, wondering if I'd come to regret my action later.

Brett blew out the breath he'd been holding, his voice as calm and steady as his mom's. "Please, Dad, let's talk about this later. I'm very thankful to have colleges interested in recruiting me for football, but I need to have a good education to fall back on when my career ends, just like you had when your football career ended. So if I don't get an offer from a school I think will give me a good education, I'll still be applying to schools without football programs."

His dad pressed his lips together in a thin line, but nodded. "Just keep an open mind, Brett."

"I am." He dug back into his breakfast, eating a bit faster than before.

Brett's twin sisters filled the silence left in the wake with their innocent, inane prattle that I found slightly amusing. It was just one notch below the annoying conversations I overheard Taylor having with her friends, but in their sweet voices, it was almost cute.

I must have been suffering from sweetness overload because with the exception of the college discussion, I was actually enjoying being part of the family. Then I reminded myself it wouldn't last, especially after I finished off the last bite of my blueberry pancakes.

When I'd arrived here this morning, I couldn't wait to leave. Now, oddly enough, I wished I could stay, and part of the reason was the guy sitting next to me. I'd found some chinks in his armor, but instead of doing a little happy dance, I felt the urge to protect him. It was like he'd trusted me with a secret, and even though I was the Queen Bitch of Eastline, I wasn't that cruel.

Especially when he'd never given me any reason to want to hurt him.

Other than dating Summer, that is.

Which, if I were to believe anything he said last night, wasn't the case.

I left the table with a full stomach and a burning in my chest that I wished I could blame on the food and thanked them for having me over.

Brett walked me to the door, following me outside. "Sorry about all that."

"It's okay."

"Yeah, but I'd really hoped my dad would take a hint and shut up." He leaned against the closed door, exhaustion lining his face. "Thanks for stopping me before I lost my cool."

I stepped closer to him, drawn to him like a moth to a bug zapper, knowing if I continued, it would only spell my doom.

But that didn't stop me.

"So, you really are human," I said in a voice so soft, I barely recognized it as my own.

He gave me a wry grin. "And you're actually capable of smiling."

He reached forward and tucked a stray strand of hair behind my ear. My heart thumped against my ribs, and I forgot how to breathe as his fingers trailed down my cheek.

"You should smile more often," he said.

"I usually don't have many reasons to smile."

"Maybe you're just not looking in the right places."

My mind grew fuzzier than the time I'd indulged in a little too much of my mom's flavored vodkas over the summer. I was slipping further under the Brett spell, and it was time to leave now before it was too late. "I'd better go, you know, before someone drives by and sees us."

"Let them." He delivered the two words in an almost challenging way.

"And what if people started talking about us?"

He shrugged. Of course it didn't matter to him. He could get away with anything he wanted at Eastline.

I was in an entirely different position. I had to work hard to maintain my position as Queen B, and the last time I'd let someone from the in-crowd get close to me, I was betrayed and humiliated. "What kind of game are you playing with me?"

He didn't answer at first. Instead, his eyes dragged up and down my body, finally coming back to my face and lingering there with an unreadable expression that made my stomach tighten. "Everyone thinks you're an evil bitch, but I've seen otherwise."

Unease wormed through my gut, up my spine and into my muscles. I just hoped he didn't see that, too. "So?"

"Why do you act that way?"

"What are you getting at?" I took a step back, raising my defenses by lining my voice with a healthy dose of acid. "Are you setting me up for some kind of intervention? Because I don't need one."

He didn't fall for it. He continued to lean against the door, calm and collected and absolutely pissing me off even more in the process. "All I'm saying is that maybe you wouldn't have to be so mean if you actually got to know people instead of writing them off as beneath you."

"I don't need this from the head of the popular crowd. You have no idea what it's like for the rest of us."

"I'm trying to lead by example, though, to keep my guys from being complete assholes, but let's face it, I'm not their mother." He pushed off the door and encroached on my space. "But if you're so determined to write me off as one of them—"

"I'm not!" My throat tightened as soon as I said the words. Damn it! "I meant, I'm not sure if you are one of them or not. For all I know, you switching places with the real person who drew my name is all part of an elaborate prank."

His eyes widened. "How—"

"I found the slip of paper with Emily's name on it the day we drew partners."

He stared at the ground, revealing nothing.

"And I don't care why you chose to help out some dipshit who didn't have the balls to work with me—"

"I did it because none of the other guys wanted to be paired up with you," he interrupted, his voice tight and quiet.

My eyes stung, and a lump formed in my throat the size of Mt. Rainier. Somewhere in the back of my mind, I'd held on to the foolish idea that he'd switched places with someone else because he wanted to work with me, because for some insane reason, he actually liked me.

I stumbled back a few more steps. "I don't need your pity."

He grabbed my arm to keep me from escaping. "It wasn't pity. I thought maybe, just maybe, if I could help you get over yourself, then life would be better for all of us."

"The only person who needs to get over himself is the conceited prick standing in front of me." I aimed for the weakest point I could find on him—the large bruise on his arm—and rammed my fist into it. He let go immediately, and I found my voice again. "And I know the perfect way to help you get off that gilded throne you're sitting on."

I held up the picture I'd taken of him earlier as I backed away, searching for some spark of fear in him. Then I turned and ran back home.

"While I appreciate the administration's efforts to prevent any harm coming to students with the installation of metal detectors at all entrances, I'd hardly call the fountain pen that was confiscated from me this morning a weapon. Unless, of course, you truly believe the pen is mightier than the sword."

The Eastline Spy
February, Junior Year

Chapter 10

By the time I got home, my pain had morphed into anger that burned in my belly and raced through my mind. It throbbed through my veins and ate away at those warm, happy feelings I'd been silly enough to feel earlier.

Pity, huh? I'd show him the meaning of pity.

I went straight to my room and paced in front of my desk, plotting my revenge. I could post the pic I got of him all over the web, on the front page of my blog, but knowing Brett, it would only backfire on me. Sure, he might get some ribbing from the guys, but all the girls would have the same reaction I did—"Aw!"

Damn, damn, damn, damn! No matter what I came up with, it couldn't hurt him. Spread a rumor that he was using performance-enhancing drugs? All he'd have to do was pee in a cup to clear his name. Photoshop him kissing Richard? No one would believe it, and I'd have Richard on my case as well.

I sank into my desk chair and massaged my temples. The truth of the matter was that I was too chicken to do something horrible to him because he really didn't deserve it. He truly was a nice guy, and that threw a kink into all my plans.

I went to my blog in the hope it would reinforce the Queen B image I was so desperately trying to maintain and remind me of how good it felt to nail someone when they'd done something wrong.

There was a comment on my most recent post that was waiting to be approved.

Dear Alexis,

> *You disappointment me. Out of all the people in the school, I thought you'd be applauding the person who revealed the cheerleading squad for the people they really are. You've always been a champion of making sure the popular kids got what they deserved.*
>
> *And they did deserve it.*
>
> *They all deserve it.*
>
> *And one day, they'll get what's coming to them.*

A chill rippled down my spine as I read it. The poster had entered "Always Watching" in the name field. I checked to see if the poster had included an email address, but that field was left blank, which was why it ended up in the moderation queue instead of going directly on the blog. I had no way of finding out who the person was, but he or she obviously had a serious grudge against the cheerleading squad.

One that seemed bigger than my own.

And based on their specific comments, he or she knew about the content of the videos. Perhaps even enough to have been the person behind them.

It was the only reason I didn't immediately delete the post. But it still didn't help me with my Brett problem.

I googled his name to see if I could dig up any dirt on him, but all I found were articles praising his prowess on the football field and how he was a top recruit in the nation.

Frigging Golden Boy.

My laptop beeped, and a window popped up saying that my dad was trying to Skype me. I opened the call request, and my dad's face filled the screen.

I'd always joked that my dad was a thinner version of Jerry Garcia with his long, frizzy gray hair and full beard. Of course, his love of the "deep insight" weed only helped with the persona. Thankfully, he wasn't high right now. "Hey, princess."

My dad was the only person who could call me princess and not lose a testicle.

"Hey, Dad."

He took one look at me and read me like an open book. "Who's pissed you off now?"

"Just a guy in my class that I'm paired up with for a project."

"Well, then, fuck him."

Tempting, but no. And with my dad, I never quite knew if he meant literally or figuratively. "It's complicated."

"How so?"

I wondered if it would be worth the awkward conversation with my dad, but I figured since he had a penis, he might have some insight into a straight guy's mind. "My head keeps telling me he's nothing but trouble, that he's just a dumb jock who's playing around with me, but there are times when I feel this overwhelming attraction to him, despite my better judgment."

"Did you sleep with him?"

94

"Dad!"

"What?"

"Ew! Even if I did—which I haven't—I wouldn't talk about sex with you."

He shrugged it off so nonchalantly I wondered if he had lit up this morning. "Sex is a perfectly natural thing, especially when there's that 'overwhelming attraction' happening."

"Says the man who screws a different graduate assistant every semester."

He gave me the "yeah, and I'm lovin' it" grin.

"But seriously, Dad, I just can't figure him out. I mean, I know I should hate him. I know I should stay far, far away from people like him. And yet, he does these nice little things like bringing me coffee—"

"Whoa, whoa, whoa—time out!" My dad made a T with his hands and held it in front of the screen until I stopped talking. "He brought you coffee?"

"Yeah, he said he thought I needed it after I'd told him I didn't sleep well the night before because of our project."

"He's totally into you, then."

"Dad, please, he's supposedly dating the head cheerleader."

"'Supposedly'?"

This was when it sucked having a professor of philosophy for a dad. He loved dissecting everything I said and throwing it back at me. "Well, he told me she wasn't his girlfriend, but Summer's draped all over him all the time like she owns him."

"And?"

"And what? Why should he be interested in me when he can have her?"

Dad crossed his arms and nodded. "And there's the root of your problem. You think you don't deserve him."

I went back to massaging my temples.

"Let me put it this way, princess—no teenage guy goes out of his way to do something nice for a girl unless he likes her."

"So?"

"So, has he done anything else you'd consider nice?"

I could still taste the blueberry pancakes from this morning. "He made me breakfast."

"Yeah, he's totally hot for you. Men won't cook for a girl unless there's sex involved. Just use a condom, okay, please? I'm not ready to become a granddad yet."

And we were back to the "ew, not going there" part of the conversation. "You have nothing to worry about in that department, Dad, because that's the extent of the moves he's made on me."

"He hasn't tried to kiss you?"

"Nope." There'd been several times when I thought he would, but I was obviously delusional.

"Touched you?"

"Not unless you count the quick feel he got when he was helping me put on a baby carrier earlier this week."

"Are you sure he's straight?"

I had to laugh at that. "Yeah, pretty sure."

Dad nodded and stroked his beard. "Then this brings up two scenarios. One—he just wants to be friends."

"Which would be a cold day in hell." Even though part of me protested when I said that. I could be friends with him— in secret, like today. But as far as school interactions went, it wasn't going to happen.

"Or he could really, really like you—like more than the 'wham, bam, thank you, ma'am' kind of way."

Sweat prickled along the back of my neck. "I can't believe I'm talking about sex and boy issues with my dad."

He snorted. "Do you think your mom would offer better

advice?"

"She'd probably tell me to start wearing makeup and dress nicer so I can fit in better with the other kids."

"Bingo. And I'm telling you to be yourself and not give a rat's ass what anyone thinks. You'll see when you get to college—all this high school clique bullshit will be gone."

"In the meantime, I'm trying to get through one more year of it without going insane." I twirled my finger in my hair, thinking about the way Brett had tucked it behind my ear earlier. "So, what should I do in the meantime?"

"Well, you could always capitalize on your attraction and jump his bones."

My head hit the desk. "Not everything can be solved with sex, Dad."

"Sure it can. Love makes the world go round, after all."

"This is not the sixties, Dad, and there are consequences to free love—like AIDS and herpes and teen pregnancy."

"Fine, but then let me ask you this—has he exposed a vulnerable part of himself to you? A secret? A weakness?"

"Maybe."

"It's yes or no, Alexis. Would he catch flack from everyone at school if they knew about it?"

I pulled up the picture of Brett with his sisters on my phone and held it up to the screen for my dad. "How about that?"

Dad nearly spewed his coffee. "You said he was a jock?"

"Star quarterback of the team."

"Does he know about the photo?"

"Yep."

"And he didn't ask you to delete it?"

"Nope."

Dad went back to stroking his beard. "Then his actions demonstrate a willingness to be intimate with you."

"We're not going back to sex again, are we?"

He shook his head. "Intimacy has to do with more than just sex, princess. It's about sharing a secret part of yourself with another person with the hope of strengthening a bond. There's a ton of literature in the philosophic community about friendship, love, and relationships, but it all touches on the importance of intimacy, even if Aristotle pooh-poohed it."

This was growing heavier with each passing second, and I wasn't ready to go there yet. "You're losing me, Professor."

"Don't play dumb with me—you know what I'm talking about. Think about you and your best friend, Morgan. You know things about her that no one else does, right?"

Sometimes far more than I wanted to. "Yeah."

"And she knows things about you that no one else does, too?"

I nodded.

"Then you two have been intimate with each other, and look how strong your friendship is. You two trust each other with your secrets, and you have a tight bond because of it." He pointed to my phone. "The fact that he allowed you to get a picture of him like that means he's trusting you in the hopes you'll return his trust and share part of yourself with him."

"Or he's trying to break down my defenses and make me vulnerable."

"Same idea, but sometimes, the road to strength goes through vulnerability and trust."

I sat for a moment, thinking about all the conversations I'd had with Brett in the last week. He was good at pushing my buttons, but maybe that was part of his agenda. The only problem was I wasn't sure what his agenda was. My conversation with my dad only left me more confused.

"Dad, why can't we have normal father–daughter

conversations that don't involve philosophy?"

"You mean like what I have with your sister? The whole 'stay away from boys or I'll get a shotgun' type?"

"How about the 'don't you dare go out in public dressed like that' type?"

That got a laugh out of my dad, especially after hearing him bitch about my sister's cheerleading uniform a few weeks ago. "So, back to the boy trouble, let me ask you this—did the things he shared with you change your opinion of him?"

"Boy, did they ever." Brett was real, with problems just like the rest of us. And yet, no matter how mad I tried to get at him, it never lingered, never developed into the long-lasting disdain I harbored for people like Summer.

"For better or worse?"

"Better, I suppose." He was smart. He had a wicked sense of humor. He had a great relationship with his sisters. He owned the football field like it was nobody's business, and yet he mentioned that he was trying to lead by example and keep the rest of the guys from being complete assholes.

"And let me guess—he scares you into doing everything you can to push him away."

I opened my mouth to tell him no, but stopped when I remember the way I'd done that very thing this morning. "How'd you guess that?"

"Because your mother does the same thing," he replied with a hint of sadness in his voice. "Listen, princess, I'm not going to tell you how to live your life, but if you let your pride build walls around you and not let anyone in, then you'll find you're going to miss out on a lot of good things in life like love and friendship. Don't be afraid to let people in."

"And what if I end up getting hurt again?"

"Well, that's part of the gamble, isn't it?" A doorbell rang off in the distance, and my dad pushed away from his desk. "I got to go—my graduate assistant is here to help me organize my notes."

I rolled my eyes. What he meant to say was that he was going to get laid. "And who is this semester's model?"

"Jackson."

That raised my brows. "Experimenting with boys?"

He snickered. "No way in hell. But I'm on sabbatical while I get my next paper written, and I figured I needed an assistant this semester who'll actually assist me."

Instead of helping him find his zipper. "Gotcha. Have fun, Dad." I was about to close the connection, but I added, "And thanks."

"Any time, princess."

The call ended, but a couple of minutes later, I got an email from my dad with the lyrics of "I Am a Rock" by Simon and Garfunkel. My dad was always sending me random song lyrics he felt were appropriate. I read through today's selection and realized how much they reminded me of the Queen B I'd become.

If you want to be happy, practice compassion. Brett's Dalai Lama quote echoed through my head. Would I be happier if I was just a bit nicer? Would it be worth the risk?

Then my gaze fell on the last two lines of "I Am a Rock" about a rock feeling no pain, and an island never crying.

Safe, but lonely, much like my place at Eastline.

"Dear Summer Hoyt, it must be nice having Mommy and Daddy replace every car you've wrecked since getting your driver's license. First, the new Camaro. Then, the new Mercedes. Now you've been downgraded to a pre-owned BMW. Oh, the horror! Maybe it's time to stop texting while driving, or you'll end up in a Honda Accord next."

The Eastline Spy
March, Junior Year

Chapter 11

Saturday night, I tossed and turned, sleeping less than when I had the stupid doll crying every few hours. My guilty conscience kept nagging me. Brett had tried to be nice to me, and I threw it back in his face. I'd even threatened to destroy his reputation to get back at him. As much as I tried to justify my actions, I couldn't. I was the Queen B, and boy, did I ever show my royal bitchiness.

I stumbled downstairs to the unfamiliar roar of the blender. My mom was using it.

I treaded carefully toward her. "Mom, are you okay?"

She looked up me with a mixture of surprise and confusion. "Yeah, why?"

"Because you're making something other than coffee in the kitchen." I sniffed it. Whatever it was smelled so awful, I couldn't begin to describe it. Let's just say the mustard-green-gray color was enough to make me want to stay away. "Please tell me you aren't going to drink that."

"Of course not, honey. It's a mask for my face." She took the blender to the sink and strained the goop into a bowl.

It was a complete one-eighty from the way Brett's mom used the sink to rinse off fruit. Even with the tense discussion about Brett's college choices, it was still a nice experience to sit down with a family over a meal.

"Mom, have you ever thought about making pancakes one morning?"

She stiffened as though she'd stuck her finger into an outlet. "You mean you want me cook breakfast?"

"Well, it would be interesting to try once."

Panic lined her pale face when she turned around. "Are you talking about microwave pancakes? Or from scratch?"

"Scratch."

Her face went another shade paler.

"Just kidding, Mom. Sorry I mentioned it." I went to the fridge and grabbed a cup of yogurt. "I'll be fine with this."

"Are you sure? I mean, I think I have a frying pan somewhere down here." She bent over to peer inside the cabinet where she kept a set of high-end cookware in a box under the counter. I think she'd maybe used it twice since she bought it five years ago.

"It's okay." I shook the yogurt container. "Like I said, I'm fine."

I retreated to my room before my mom offered to let me try out her new mask.

I decided I needed to talk to people who had some clue of what life was like at Eastline, but I knew Morgan would only greet me with a string of cuss words if I dared to call her before noon. Thankfully, I had my copy of *Pride and Prejudice* to distract me while I was waiting. I lost myself in the world of manners and miscommunication, of country dances and grand Regency balls. But this time, the familiar pages didn't comfort me like they usually did. Instead, I kept hearing Richard telling me I was too proud to admit I liked Brett and my dad telling me my walls of pride were keeping me from enjoying life.

And then it hit me.

I was Mr. Fucking Darcy.

I'd been so busy setting myself above the rest of my classmates because I thought I was better than them that I refused to see any good in them. And there was Brett, whom I'd judged based on his association with his bonehead peers (like Sanchez), reaching out to me and trying to show me that he was different from the rest, but I'd been the asshole who rebuked him.

I closed the book and threw it on my bed. Damn it! When did my life get so frigging complicated?

Oh, yeah, the day Brett decided to switch places with someone else so he could help me "get over" myself.

I grabbed my phone and called Richard. "I'm ready for my intervention, Dr. Phil."

"Not at ten in the morning, sweetie," he replied, his voice slurred with sleep. "This diva still needs at least two more hours of beauty rest."

"Fine, but can you and Morgan meet me at the fro-yo place at two?"

"Me and Morgan?" His voice perked up. "Damn, you must need some serious help."

"*Serious* doesn't begin to describe it."

***

"I think I screwed up—badly." I stood in front of my two best friends like a convicted criminal at his sentencing and waited for them to pass judgment.

Instead, Richard passed me a waffle cup of mocha frozen yogurt topped with chocolate chips, brownie bits, and a dollop of marshmallow cream. "Sit down and tell us about it."

I chose to grab a couple bites of sugar-laden courage before I spilled my guts. "I've been a complete bitch."

"Tell us something we don't know," Morgan said dryly, cocking one brow up.

"No, this goes beyond my normal bitchiness."

"And something tells me it has to do with what you did with Mr. Quarterback after the game." Richard held his spoon up to the corner of his mouth, trying to look innocent while the intelligence in his eyes saw straight through me.

I checked the shop to make sure no one was around to overhear my confession. Then I took a deep breath. "It does."

Richard jumped up from his chair, pointing his spoon at me. "Ha, I told you so! Pay up, Morgan."

"Oh my God—you two were betting on me?"

"Unfortunately." Morgan reached into her wallet and tossed a twenty to Richard. "I didn't think you'd be caught dead with him outside of school, but I guess I was wrong."

"So, spill," Richard said as he tucked the money into his shirt pocket. "What did you two kids do after the game?"

"Argue." I ate a few more bites to let them stew as payback for betting on me like that. "He dumped the doll on me the rest of the night so he could go somewhere with Summer."

Morgan shook her head. "What an ass."

Richard nodded, licking the frozen yogurt off his spoon and shivering. "Yes, what an ass, but I think we're talking about two different things."

I rolled my eyes. "I thought this was an intervention, not a drool over Brett's behind get-together."

"Sorry, sweetie, but I have to get the visual out of my mind if you want me to get truly angry on your behalf." He posed like he was meditating in a yoga class for close to a minute before saying, "Okay, mind cleared. Back to your issues."

"So when I got upset for him dumping the project on me so he could bang his girlfriend, he said she wasn't his girlfriend and—"

"Hold on," Morgan interrupted. "Summer's not his girlfriend?"

She and Richard exchanged glances and said in unison, "Fuck buddies."

"That's what I thought, too, but when I went over to his house the next morning, I—"

"Wait." Now it was Richard's turn to interrupt me. "You went over to his house? Mind sharing those coordinates with me sometime so I can stalk him?"

I stabbed my fro-yo with my spoon. "Will you two please let me finish?"

"I'm sorry, Alexis, but this is the juiciest gossip I've heard in months." Richard leaned forward on the table, his chin in his hands. "Keep going—I'm listening."

"I only agreed to take the doll Friday night because he said he'd take it all weekend. I went to his house to drop it off and found him playing with his sisters, and it was so…"

My voice caught. I usually wasn't at a loss for words, but as I pictured the scene with him and the twins, a storm of emotions rolled through me. Envy. Amusement. Frustration. It reminded me of what my family had been like before my parents split, what I wished I could have again. It showed me a different side to the normally cool and collected Brett. And it made me wonder why I'd stayed afterward since it only ended up backfiring on me.

"Cute," I said at last.

Morgan made a gagging gesture with her spoon. "I'd have to see it to believe it, and even if I did, I might get ill."

I had proof on my camera, but I decided not to show her. If Brett was trusting me with the fact he let his little sisters ride on his back like a horse, then I could keep his secret.

At least for now.

Until he really pissed me off.

"But yeah, when I tried to drop the doll off, he invited me to stay for breakfast."

"He what?" Morgan's eyes widened. "You do realize you're the first person I've heard of who got invited to spend more than five minutes in his house, right?"

I choked on my mocha chocolate chip. "I find that highly unbelievable."

"It's true," Morgan continued. "I had algebra with Kaitlyn Matsumura, and she used to complain about how he'd meet her at the door and go. I think in the three months they dated, she only met his sister once, and she never met his parents."

Kaitlyn was one of the popular girls Brett had dated briefly during our sophomore year before he became the über-football star, before Summer had set her sights on him and scared the other girls away. Kaitlyn ended up transferring later that year, but I'd never heard about the reason she and Brett broke up. I'd always assumed it was because he went after greener pastures—in this case, Summer.

"So I wonder why he invited me over."

"Obviously not for your fashion sense." Richard pointed to the My Little Pony on today's T-shirt, his nose wrinkled. "I think our next intervention needs to be in wardrobe."

"Are you offering makeover services?" Morgan teased.

"Oh, please, I'm gay, but I don't give makeovers. However,

I do think Alexis needs to dress in something other than what a five-year-old would wear."

"Please, you two, focus. I'm getting to the meat of the story."

"Ooh, she said *meat*." Richard wiggled in his chair. "So did you two go up to his room and get all hot and heavy?"

"Nowhere even close to that."

"You disappoint me." Morgan gave me a playful pout. "So, are his parents vampires or something?"

"No, they're actually quite normal. His sisters, too. Nothing strange there." Although now I was wondering why he brought me to breakfast and not his old girlfriend. "He even made delicious blueberry pancakes."

"Are you sure you didn't bump your head and dream all this up, à la Dorothy in the *Wizard of Oz*?" Richard asked, his mouth hanging open.

I shook my head. "And after we ate, he mentioned that he liked seeing me smile."

"So did you ask him to publicly dump Summer?" Morgan asked. "Because that would make me smile, and I'm not even into him."

Richard smacked her arm. "Stop being so evil for a moment and let's help Alexis dissect that statement. So, I take it you weren't all in your Royal Bitchiness mode during breakfast."

I shook my head. "And I actually found myself laughing with him and his sisters."

"Which meant he found a way to get under your armor."

I opened my mouth and shut it right away. Was that what he meant when he said he saw I wasn't a complete bitch?

"Uh-oh, our Queen B went soft on us," Morgan said, exchanging worried glances with Richard. "Do we need to remind you why we hate him and everyone else in his crowd?"

"But that's the thing—I don't think he's like the others."

"Bullshit." Morgan shoved her half-eaten cup of frozen yogurt away from her. "He's screwing Summer, isn't he?"

I hesitated. "I'm not entirely sure."

"Of course he is. Guys our age will screw anything that stands still long enough, present company excluded."

"No offense taken," Richard said, scraping his cup clean. "If it doesn't have a penis, I'm not interested."

"He's totally playing you, Alexis." Morgan leaned forward, her eyes narrowed. "Think about it—he switched places to work with you because he knew you'd get all anal-retentive about it and he'd get a good grade on the project from you doing the brunt of the work."

"That's not the reason he gave when I asked him about it." A sharp pain filled my chest as I said the words. Even now, his admission still stung.

Morgan backed away, mocking shock stretching her face. "Oh? And what reason did he give?"

I swirled the chocolate chips and what was left of the marshmallow cream into my yogurt. "He said he did it because he wanted to help me get over myself."

"What. A. Fucking. Asshole," Morgan said loud enough to earn a glare from a mother with several small children at her table. "He's going down after that. What shall we do to show him that if anyone needs to get over themselves, it's him?"

A couple of weeks ago, I would've been the first person to hop onto Morgan's revenge bandwagon with an exposé on my blog, but now I wasn't so sure I wanted to go down that path. At least, not with him. Yes, I was hurt and angry and wanted to grab him by the hair and bang his head against the wall until I'd rattled the frustration out of my system. But something held me back. I wished to God I knew what it was, but I couldn't name it.

Maybe I was going soft.

If so, I was screwed.

The sharp jangle of the bell on the door pulled me from my thoughts, and my heart hardened with hatred when I saw Summer Hoyt coming in.

Nope, I wasn't going completely soft.

She stopped just inside the door and stared at me through heavy lidded eyes as though she was deciding if she wanted to patronize the same place I'd desecrated.

I met her gaze, daring her to come closer.

Several seconds stretched by, each one reminding me of how good it felt to be a Queen B, of how much I enjoyed the power I wielded against the superficial and obscene in our high school like Summer. I forgot all about Brett Pederson and my doubts. Right now, I had no desire to get over myself. I was relishing my crown instead.

One corner of Summer's mouth rose into a smirk, and she pulled out her phone. A moment later, she said in her sugary-sweet slut voice, "Brett, honey, I'm at the fro-yo shop, and I was wondering if you wanted me to get anything for you?"

My throat started to close in a moment of what I could only assume was jealousy. I took a deep breath, swallowed past it, and continued to stare her down.

Her smirk widened into a "screw you" grin. "Of course. How about I bring it by your place so we can enjoy it together?"

"So that's how she convinces guys to spend time with her," I said to Morgan and Richard. "Bribery."

"Gee, and I always thought it was because she put out," Morgan replied.

Summer's lips fell, and it was my turn to give the "up yours" grin as I overheard her say, "But we never spend time at your—"

"I told you so," Morgan whispered.

"Fine, I'll meet you at the park." When Summer caught the three of us hanging on every word of her conversation, she straightened her shoulders and added in a voice reserved for D-grade porn, "Maybe we can take a little walk and get lost for a while. I know a very private place we can go to for a little fun."

She hung up a second later, but the damage had been done. For the first time, I was beginning to believe that maybe there wasn't anything going on between Brett and Summer. And even if there was, she was obviously desperate for more.

Morgan silently dared me to mention breakfast at Brett's house so Summer could overhear, but I remained silent. Until I was certain of his motives, I was going to keep what happened yesterday morning to my tiny circle of friends.

However, my best friend wasn't content to keep that information to herself. Morgan's jaw hardened, and she looked at me as though I'd lost my mind. "So Brett makes really good blueberry pancakes, huh?" she asked loud enough for Summer to hear.

The head cheerleader froze, her spoonful of gummy bears hovering over her mountain of vanilla frozen yogurt.

I kicked Morgan under the table.

She yelped and reached down to rub her shins, but it was too late. She'd let my secret out, and by tomorrow, the whole school would know I had breakfast with Brett.

Correction—that Brett had made me breakfast.

All I could do now was go with it and take advantage of the situation. "Yep. He even flips them in air as he cooks them."

Summer tossed the spoon on the counter, completely missing the container of gummy bears, and stomped off to the register to pay for her yogurt. She was breathing hard like she'd just completed a series of high kicks, a flush of color in her cheeks. Then she stormed out of the fro-yo place and tore out of the parking lot with such urgency, her BMW left skid marks on the pavement.

Morgan collapsed into laughter, banging her fist on the table. "That was awesome!"

"Why did you do that?" I asked, gripping the table to keep from smacking her on the back of the head.

She wiped the corners of her eyes. "Why didn't you?"

"Because maybe I wanted to keep that information private."

"And miss out on a chance to throw it in Summer's face?" She pointed to the still-warm tread marks outside. "Did you see her face when she put it all together and realized you'd done something with Brett that she hadn't?"

I blew a breath and released the table. "Okay, fine, yes, it was pretty damn funny to see her lose her shit."

"It was like the best moment of our senior year so far."

"Want to know what I found funny about all that?" Richard point to the abandoned cup of mocha flavored frozen yogurt on the counter. "It seems Miss Thang was in such a hurry to leave, she forgot Brett's fro-yo."

"How do you know it wasn't hers?" I asked, refusing to believe Brett liked the same flavor I did.

"Because while you were getting all Clint Eastwood on Summer, I was actually listening to the other end of the conversation." He flicked his ears. "These babies heard every word Brett said."

Part of me wanted to know, but I was too busy riding the high I got from winning this showdown with my arch nemesis to ask right now.

Morgan pulled out her phone and began typing. "I have the perfect meme for this. I'll post it to Tumblr when I get home." She slid out from her seat and headed for the door, not looking up from her phone. "Just keep doing what you're doing, and don't let me down, Alexis. And we're still on for Tuesday at The Purple Dog, right?"

She was gone before I could tell her I wasn't finished yet, but I already knew what she'd say. *Forget about Brett. He's not worth worrying over. He won't even bother speaking to you once the project is over. That's just how people like him are. High school sucks, but it will be over soon. Focus on college guys.*

Except as I glanced across the table at Richard, I saw I wasn't the only one left with more questions than answers. He started with pointing at my half-eaten bowl and asking, "Are you going to finish that?"

"No," I said slowly. "Why?"

"Because I'm still hungry." He grabbed it and took a bite. How he remained rail thin when he ate like that was beyond my understanding. "That's not the only leftovers I'd be interested in, if you know what I mean."

A group of popular kids from the class below me invaded the shop. I took that as my cue to get going. "Need a ride?"

"Puh-lease." He grabbed the yogurt and took it with him, still stuffing his face as he added, "I suppose if I have to bum a ride off someone, at least it's with you."

"Still no car from grandma yet?" I asked as we walked out.

"Getting closer." He slid into the passenger seat. "I overheard her asking my dad if he thought I'd like her old Lexus."

"And would you?"

"Hello? It's a car! And it has leather with heated seats. Do you realize all the naughty thoughts that are going through my head when it comes to that?"

"No, not really." And I really hoped he wouldn't follow Morgan's lead and jump onto the TMI train.

Richard waited until we were out of the parking lot before he spoke, all sass gone from his voice. "So, I take it we weren't finished with the intervention, were we?"

"Not even close." I tapped my fingers on the steering wheel. Should I even push the issue?

Richard decided to do it for me. "Well, then, let me point out a few things you might have missed, sweetie. First off, all the world's a stage, and all the men and women merely players."

"Thank you, William Shakespeare."

"You're totally welcome, and yes, I freely admit to being a player in every sense of the word, but that's not where I'm going. What I mean to say is that we've all been cast in roles for this *High School Musical* wannabe. You're the token Mean Girl."

"I prefer Queen Bitch."

"Same thing. I'm the token Gay Guy, Morgan's the token Goth Girl, Summer the Brainless Head Cheerleader, Brett the Superman Football Hero, etc. But that's not who we really are."

"If you're going to start singing show tunes, I'm stopping the car right now and kicking you to the curb."

"Oh, sweetie, if I wanted to torture you, I'd go all Justin Bieber on you."

"Ack, don't!" I feigned horror in between chuckles. "But since you actually sounded serious at first, I'll let you continue."

"All I'm saying is that while we're at Eastline, we settle into our little niches and act the way everyone expects us to act, but sometimes, that's just not enough. I mean, yes, I'm glad to be the token Gay Guy. I'm glad I came out for everyone to see. I'm glad I'm not living in shame of my sexuality and trying to fake being all macho just so I can be one of the boys. And I'm glad that most of the students are cool with me being gay. But with that comes the fact no one really takes me seriously."

"Are you sure none of that has to do with the fact you tried out for the cheerleading squad last year?"

"Oh, that was just a bit of fun. And it's all part of my token Gay Guy persona. I'm catty and the life of a party and gayer than life, and that's fine—I have fun going to the extremes. People expect that from me, and it, you know, makes them more comfortable with the fact I like penis. But if I tried to discuss the Declaration of Independence with someone in AP Government, do you think they'd listen to what I have to say? What if I'd tried out for the debate team instead of the cheerleading squad? Do you see what I mean?"

I stopped at a red light and let what he'd said sink in. "So, are you accusing me of using my Queen Bitch persona as a shield because I'm too chicken-shit to be myself?"

"You said it, not me." He looked out the window as the light changed. "Look at Morgan. We both know she acts the way she does to rebel against her parents. It's a little immature, but it keeps her from dealing with them. And let's face it, they are a messed-up pair. She'll be so much healthier mentally once she moves away from home."

"Agreed."

"But I don't know if you've noticed lately, but she's calming down a bit. She hasn't screwed Stupid Surfer Boy yet, for example."

"Thank God."

He turned back to me. "You got that 'ew!' vibe from him, too? I mean, what is she thinking? He's so not her type. He reeks of Frat Boy."

"Stereotyping, are we?"

"In his case, yes." A few seconds passed as Richard grew serious again. "But back to where I was going with my Dr. Phil moment—you have a chance to do something most of us only dream of."

"And what's that? Eat blueberry pancakes with Brett Pederson?"

"I was going to suggest something else, but that would totally throw me from this rare moment of maturity. What I'm trying to say is that you can break the mold and shake things up in this upper middle class suburbia hellhole."

My palms grew sweaty just thinking about where he was going. "By doing what?"

"You and Brett—the Mean Girl and the Quarterback, the Queen B and the Homecoming King. Think of the possibilities there, Alexis."

"We are so not couple material," I said quickly enough for even my airhead sister to have recognized the denial behind my words if she'd heard me.

"You were the one he invited over to have breakfast with his family."

We pulled into Richard's driveway right behind a gold Lexus sedan. Must've been his grandmother's car.

But Richard didn't make the slightest move to get out. He stared at me, drumming his fingers on his lap. Like the good friend he was, he wasn't leaving until I'd unburdened my soul.

"Fine. So when Brett admitted that one of the reasons he

switched places with the person who drew my name was to help me get over myself, I sort of lost it and told him I didn't need his pity. I even threatened to post a picture of him on my blog that would seriously damage his reputation."

"Uh-huh," he said, nodding.

"But in truth, I was freaking out because I got to see a side of him I didn't know existed, and then he said he liked seeing me smile, which I interpreted as he sort of liked me, but I was too proud to even consider going out with him because we're so different, but in truth we're really not that different, and oh my God, I've fucked up."

I was panting by the time I finished my confession. If I'd been Catholic, I'd probably have been clutching my rosary on the other side of the screen waiting for the priest to deliver my penance. Instead, I had the venerable Richard offering counsel.

He steepled his fingers in front of his mouth, trying to appear grim even though his lips twitched with amusement. "So why did you need me again? It sounds like you already know what you did and what you need to do."

I leaned my head back against the seat, staring at the ceiling. Yeah, I knew what I'd done. I'd taken Brett's act of kindness and thrown it back in his face. "How the hell can I fix things without apologizing? Before last week, I wouldn't have even considered doing that, but every time I think about the way he looked at me when he said he liked seeing me smile—"

My voice broke, and bitterness filled my mouth. "It's just not going to happen, okay?"

"You know, you're getting too hung up on the sex thing."

"Excuse me?"

"I can see it in your eyes. Let me guess, when you two had that 'moment,' you were alone?"

"Yes."

Richard leaned over. "And he was standing close to you?"

"Yes."

"And you probably thought he was going kiss you, right?"

"How—never mind." I closed my eyes and banged my head on my seat. "Yes, I thought he was. But he didn't."

He waited a beat, his eyes showing that he understood my frustration better than I thought he would. Then he cracked a smile that didn't reach the pain lingering in his eyes. "You really need to do something about that sexual frustration of yours. Maybe we can get Morgan to recommend a good vibrator, and you can nickname it 'Brett.'"

My face burned. I'd opened up to him and confessed, and now he was taking the piss out of me for it. "Shut the fuck up."

Richard backed away, laughing. "And while you're considering getting on your knees to grovel and apologize, you might consider throwing in a blow job to sweeten the deal."

I wrapped my fingers around the steering wheel to keep from wrapping them around his throat. "Get the hell out of my car now."

"I was just trying to lighten up the mood."

"Well, you only made it worse, so get out."

"Okay, okay, sorry. But let me ask you this—have you ever considered just being friends with him? I mean, yes, there would always be that underlying sexual tension, but at least you could still have breakfast with him on the weekends without the entire school knowing about it and maybe see if he's worth the risk."

"The risk of what?"

"Of breaking the mold." Richard finally opened the door and got out of the car, never breaking eye contact with me.

"Just between you and me, I think you two would be an awesome power couple."

He slammed the door shut. "Thanks for the ride."

I drove home, wondering if Brett would be worth the risk—not only breaking the mold, but for showing him myself.

Chapter 12

I woke up Monday morning still debating if I should apologize to Brett.

By the time I got to school, I had my answer.

Brett stood by my locker, chatting with a couple of his friends. As soon as he saw me, he gave me the doll, his face cold and unreadable, and left without saying a word.

Yeah, I'd really screwed up.

A steel rod of indignation kept my head held high, though. If that was the way he wanted it to be, then so be it. I didn't need him. And once we were done with this project, I wouldn't have to interact with him for the rest of the school year.

Just the way I liked it.

Except, when I sat down at my table during health class, I

was alone.

Brett had chosen to go back to his original seat in the front of the class with Sanchez.

My stomach sank as the bell rang and Mr. DePaul started talking about the effect of stress on the body. I unstrapped the doll carrier and laid it to the side so I could take notes, but my head really wasn't into the lecture. For someone who hadn't had to share a table with anyone since her sophomore year, I actually missed Brett's constant interruptions. They made this ridiculous class more bearable.

How far was I willing to go to get him back to my table? Obviously, I had to offer him something. It wasn't prime real estate as far as getting noticed by the teacher went, which could actually be a perk. I'd even be willing to smile once in a while if it meant he kept me from drooling on my laptop as I was nodding off to sleep.

But apologize? Maybe, if I absolutely had to.

I zoned out as I tried to find a way to entice Brett back without jeopardizing my "niche." I could text him. Slip him a note. Offer him a can of Red Bull with the next baby exchange. Offer to take the doll on Thursday night so he could rest up for the game (that was pushing it, though, because that meant I'd be on board with the whole "Go, Team!" agenda).

When I came out of my head, Mr. DePaul was pointing to things on a table. I read the title. *Stress Scale for Teens.* Then I scanned the list. No wonder I wanted to stay home sick most days.

Or why I felt sick to my stomach as I struggled over this whole Brett issue.

"And since you can see that an unplanned pregnancy and fathering a child are significantly stressful events that can affect your health, I decided to keep you paired up with your baby partners for this week's assignment."

While the rest of the class groaned, my heart quickened. That meant I'd have to work with Brett again. I wouldn't have to come up with some lame excuse to get back in his company.

I waited for him to look back at me, to acknowledge that we'd be paired up a bit longer, but he didn't. He kept his eyes fixed on the PowerPoint screen.

Mr. DePaul went to his computer and clicked a button. Two seconds later, I got an email with this week's assignment. Stress inventory and strategies for coping.

The bell rang. My heart thudded at a surprisingly slow and steady beat that was in stark contrast to my shaking hands. I forced myself to stay seated and take my time putting away my laptop while Brett whispered something to Sanchez.

A full minute passed before he came my way. He pulled out one of the chairs from the row in front of me and sat down, his elbows resting on the table. "So, when would be a good time to get together for this?"

"You mean you want to work together?"

"It's not like DePaul left us any choice on the matter." He leveled his gaze with me, carrying a new hard edge to his words that he didn't have before.

Not that I blamed him. Once bitten and all that.

I checked the email. "The stress evaluation is due Wednesday morning."

"Can we meet up tomorrow after class?"

I shook my head, thankful I'd agreed to meet Morgan at the Purple Dog tomorrow. "I have plans."

He ran his fingers through his hair as though I was the most exasperating person he knew.

Perhaps I was. I know he was for me.

"I'm done for the rest of the day," I offered. "We can work

on it now, if you'd like."

I was trying to be nice for once. This wasn't so bad. Baby steps.

"Sure, I'm done, too. Want to meet up in the library?"

And then my gut clamped down and my mouth dried up. "Um, can we meet somewhere a little less public?"

Suspicion filled his dark eyes. "Why?"

"You know why."

He relaxed, the tension leaving his mouth free to form a semblance of a smile. "Then where do you want to meet up? My place is a zoo since the twins are still at home with my mom."

"My place will be empty. Does that sound okay with you?"

Something else flickered in his eyes, but not suspicion this time. It was hot and primal and completely melted my insides. As quickly as it appeared, though, it was gone.

He rose from his chair. "Can I meet you there in an hour? I promised Summer I'd meet her for lunch."

I nodded. "I'll text you my address."

"Thanks." I expected him to leave, but he lingered there in front of me for a whole minute, staring at me as though he wasn't quite sure he could trust me.

I didn't dare look away. If he was testing me, I refused to buckle. I crossed my arms (a great way to hide a pair of shaking hands while still appearing tough) and added a jolt of intimidation to my gaze.

At last, he turned around. "See you in a bit."

As soon as he was out of sight and the room was empty, I fell apart. I leaned over the table, sucking in deep breaths like an asthmatic trying to open up her airways. My heart pounded so hard, its vibrations shook my entire body.

I'd been given a second chance.

I just hoped it wouldn't come back to bite me in the ass.

***

The jock *would* drive a gas-guzzling black 4Runner.

I watched through the blinds as Brett drove up, got out of the car, and checked something on his phone multiple times. His eyes flickered between it and my front door as he strolled up the walkway, oblivious of how he was putting my reputation in jeopardy.

I opened the door before he had a chance to knock. "Come in before someone sees you."

"Why didn't you tell me you lived just around the corner from me?"

I shut the door and peeked through the blinds again to make sure no one else was around. "I thought you might have picked up on it when I left on foot Saturday."

"Hey, for all I knew, you had parked down the street because you were scared to be seen with me."

My spine bristled. "I'm not scared to be seen with you."

"Then why are you acting all paranoid like now?" He caught my hand as I was in the process of closing all the blinds.

A zing of something—anger, attraction, I couldn't tell—raced up my arm. I yanked my hand back. "I just think we shouldn't be seen together outside of school."

"Why?" He closed in on me as he waited for my response.

"Because," was all I managed to say. Anything more would reveal the way my voice trembled from the increased skipping of my heart.

He invaded my personal space even more, a grin playing on those perfect lips. "Because you're scared of something, right?"

"Only of people getting the wrong idea."

"About what?"

"Us." I turned around and added some distance between us. My pulse slowed with each blessed step I took. "The kitchen's this way."

He dawdled, taking his time to look around my house. I could only imagine how he viewed it. Everything was neat, spotless, organized. It looked like one of those photo spreads for a home magazine. "Nice place."

"Thanks," I replied, not knowing how to interpret his compliment.

"Did you just move in?"

"No."

"Then why aren't there any family pictures or, you know, evidence that this is your house?"

"My mom isn't big on hanging pictures." Unless they were of her. Unfortunately, the shortest path to the kitchen crossed in front of the shrine to my mom's beauty pageant days.

And, of course, Brett would stop there. He stared at the glass cabinet full of tiaras, sashes, and photos. "Is that your mom?" he asked, pointing to the glossy eight by ten of her in the Miss America pageant.

"Yes."

His eyes widened. "Wow."

"Don't you dare call her hot or sexy or a MILF."

"Well, you have to admit, she was pretty good looking." He peered closer at the photo. "Miss Vermont, huh?"

"Yes." I kept my voice flat and bored, even though I wanted to drag him away from the cabinet. I was just grateful my mom wasn't here to pull out her tiaras and parade around the room for him like she'd done for my friends in the past.

At last, he stepped back. "Well, that explains Taylor."

"What is that supposed to mean?"

"You know—the eyeliner emergencies, the fear of having

a loose strand of hair from her ponytail." He rolled his eyes. "You have no idea how many of those conversations I've had to listen to between her and Summer."

"I can only imagine." And thank my lucky stars she'd never come to me for those issues. I jerked my head toward the kitchen. "And now that you've stopped gawking at my mom, let's get working on the assignment."

He looked at me like he was trying to figure out where I fit in my dysfunctional family. "It also kind of explains you, too."

I counted to ten as I exhaled. Would it be worth touching him to drag him away from the glittering Bimbo Award Center? I settled for snapping my fingers in front of his face. "Brett, please, I didn't invite you here to psychoanalyze me or my family. Assignment, remember?"

He finally followed me into the kitchen and set his bag on the glossy cherry wood table, pulling out his laptop. It was probably the first time the table had been used in months. We normally ate at the island on the barstools, if we sat down to eat at all. The twice-weekly maids had polished the nearly new table to a mirror shine this morning.

I went to the fridge. "Do you want something to drink?" I scanned the almost-bare shelves. "We've got soy milk, pomegranate juice, and chardonnay." I pulled out the half-empty bottle of wine and gave it a playful little shake for him.

"Trying to get me drunk so you can take advantage of me?"

"You wish." Although the thought was more tempting than I cared to admit.

He laughed, and some of the knots in my stomach unraveled. I may not have been making blueberry pancakes, but I was on my way to recapturing that easy feeling I experienced with him Saturday morning before I learned I was his pity project.

"Water will be fine," he replied.

I poured two glasses and brought them to the table.

Brett had already moved his laptop next to mine and pulled up the assignment. "So, we need to do a stress assessment that's due Wednesday morning and a stress modification work plan that's due Friday. Piece of cake."

"Except we're also juggling Junior, too." I nodded to the doll that lay on the other end of the table.

"Ah, come on, Lexi. It's not that hard."

Junior chose that moment to prove him wrong by screaming at the top of his electronic lungs.

Like a pro, Brett jumped up from his chair, scooped the doll up in his arms, and whipped out the bottle. A few seconds later, the doll was quiet.

I have no idea how long my mouth was hanging open before I caught myself, but judging by the amusement in Brett's eyes, he'd seen it. "How did you know what to do?" I asked.

"That was the 'I'm hungry' cry. The 'I'm dirty' cry is lower pitched."

Once again, I had to convince myself that Brett wasn't perfect. "And you figured this out how?"

"By listening." The doll stopped making the sucking sounds, which prompted Brett to place the doll against his chest and gently pat its back. A few seconds later, a contented burp signaled that Junior would be silent for the next couple of hours. "Okay, back to the project."

He slid back into the chair next to me, and a new sense of awareness smacked me. Yes, Brett was hot. Yes, he smelled good and had a great body and made my hormones do insane things. Yes, he drove me crazy by not cowering before me like most of the people in the school. But now I was beginning to realize he might be smarter than I gave him credit for.

And if I was beginning to think of him as something other than a dumb jock, I was in danger of getting in way over my head.

High school boys were supposed to be immature idiots, right?

Brett started going down the list of teen stressors, starting with the items with the highest scores. "Well, neither one of us has lost a parent recently. We haven't had an unplanned pregnancy."

"Unless you count Junior there."

He cracked a grin. "Fair enough."

We went down the list until he came to the item worth sixty-seven points. "Change in acceptance by peers," he murmured. "Is that why you're so anal about not being seen with me?"

"Bingo, Einstein."

"Why?"

"What do you mean, why?"

"I mean most girls in the school would *like* to be seen with me." He could have said that in an arrogant, preening way, but instead, his words were matter-of-fact.

"If by most girls, you mean Summer, then yes, I suppose you're right. But I'm not like most girls."

"No shit."

I rolled my eyes toward him. "Is there a reason why you're sidetracking me from the assignment?"

He rested his chin in his palm, his eyes never wavering from me. "I think you're scared that if people saw us hanging out together, they'd realize that maybe you aren't quite the bitch they think you are."

He was absolutely correct on one count, but I wasn't going

to let him know that. Or the fact that, you know, I might actually like him in that hot and horny teenage way. Or maybe even in the "I might actually consider going out with you someday" way. "More like they'd wonder if you'd been hit in the head one too many times during football practice."

"So you're more worried about my reputation?" He covered his heart with his hand, sarcasm dripping from his voice. "I'm so touched."

"Do you want me to kick you out of my house?"

He shook his head, grinning the whole time in a way that left little prickles of sweat along the back of my neck. "Don't worry, Lexi—your secret is safe with me."

"And what secret is that?" I pretended to stare at my screen, even though I was watching him out of the corner of my eye.

He leaned over, giving my rebellious hormones an unwelcome surge when the heat of his skin radiated onto mine. "That you're actually capable of being nice and braiding ribbons into little girls' hair instead of being the ball-busting bitch you want everyone to see you as."

I clenched my hands into fists to keep them from shaking and remembered I still had the picture of him playing horsey with his sisters. "Are you asking for a demonstration of the latter?"

He shook his head, settling into his seat again. "Nope. I've already seen enough through your blog."

"I suppose you're getting a rise out of tormenting me, aren't you?"

His grin only confirmed it, even though he said nothing.

I scanned the list, looking for distraction in any place I could find it. "Here's one for you—breaking up with a girlfriend."

"Not an issue."

"Oh, yeah, I forgot, Summer's not your girlfriend, even though she tells everyone in the school she is."

That wiped the grin off his face. "She does?"

"How clueless are you? She even sent me threats through my sister to keep my hands off of you."

His brows bunched together, accentuating the downward turn of his mouth. "Perhaps I need to have a little talk with her."

"Go right ahead. Meanwhile, I'm giving you points for the breakup since in some respects, you are having to end this fictitious relationship Summer's created." I jotted down the number, daring to give voice to the question that had been lingering in my mind since I'd first acknowledged my attraction to him. "So, what is the story between you two?"

"I could ask you the same thing."

"She's a deceptive, superficial, manipulative, back-stabbing bitch."

He let out a low whistle. "Sounds like there's a story there."

"I'll share if you will."

"I'm game." He cracked his knuckles. "I know Summer wants to be more than friends, but I'm not into her."

"What are you into?"

His eyes flickered over me, his grin widening. "That's not part of our deal."

My cheeks burned, and I stayed focused on my screen. "Fine. But then tell me this—if you know she's into you even though you're not, why do you hang out with her all the time?"

He tapped his pen on the table, his lips pursed. "Maybe because I know her better than you, and I know she could really use a friend. She's not as perfect as she pretends to be. It's all an act to protect her from what's really going on."

"Meaning?"

He stilled. "How well do you know Summer?"

"Apparently not well enough, since she was the one person who betrayed me."

"Aha. I knew there was a history between you two."

Flashbacks of that day raced through my mind, each one accompanied by a fresh wave of nausea. Summer standing on a chair in the center of the lunchroom, my stolen diary in her hand. Her voice, as loud as it was on the football field, reading each embarrassing line I'd written. The laughter that followed after each secret confession of my soul. The pointed fingers, snickers, and names that tormented me for the months that followed. The dark nights where I'd cry myself to sleep and pray for some serious illness so I wouldn't have to go back to school the next morning.

"Just don't share any secrets with her unless you want them broadcasted to the entire school," I said, my voice hoarse.

One brow raised, but he said nothing.

I kept going down the list, acutely aware of the silence that bordered on pity. "Hey, at least neither one of us has been suspended from school or had a parent recently incarcerated."

"Yeah, I suppose that's true." Then he grew quiet again, his mouse arrow hovering over the line that listed the value for "increased arguments between/with parents."

His unease was infectious, worming through my stomach and twitching into my legs. But since he felt like he had every right to psychoanalyze me, I figured I could return the favor. "So, your dad's really pushing you hard for that football scholarship, huh?"

He pushed back from the table and stood, turning his back to me.

Now he knew what it felt like when someone pointed out

his issues.

"I suppose you might understand," he started, then clamped up. He reached into his bag and pulled out a football.

Geez, did he lose part of his super jock mojo if he was more than ten feet away from one of those things?

I could have been completely snarky and told him to stay the hell out my problems if he didn't want me returning the favor, but I couldn't make my tongue form those words. Because perhaps I did understand. And because perhaps learning more about the real Brett intrigued me. "What?"

He squeezed the ball in his hands, his fingers splayed between the laces. "My dad played football. He even got to play in the NFL for a couple of years until he blew his knee out. And since I'm his only son, he's been pushing football on me as long as I can remember."

Now it was my turn to lean my cheek against my hand and study the person in the hot seat. "Do you even like playing football?"

"Are you kidding? I love it." He pretended to pass the ball, the lean muscles of his body moving with the same fluid grace as they had on Friday night. "I love the intensity, the strategy, the physicality, the camaraderie of the team."

"Do you really mean that, or are you just trying to incorporate your SAT flash cards into a sentence?"

He slapped the football, a single note of laughter breaking free. "Maybe both?"

"I thought as much."

"But in all honesty, I do enjoy playing. What I don't like is the fact my dad keeps trying to make it the only thing in my life. I mean, yeah, it would be great if I could play college ball and get a free ride because of it, but my mom is also right in that I need to make sure I have a back-up plan."

"And what would you do if you didn't have football?"

He stared the ball for several long seconds as through I was asking him to kill an old friend. "I have a few ideas, but nothing definite."

"Meaning?" He was hiding something from me, something he didn't want me to know about. And the way he kept dancing around on his feet told me he was struggling with whether to reveal his secret to me.

"Meaning I'll explore them once I get closer to Signing Day. If I get any offers, then I'll look at their programs and see which one feels like the best fit and make my decision then."

"The football programs or the academic programs?"

"Both." He finally looked over to me. "What about you? What do you want to do with your life?"

"I'm seventeen, Brett. I have no friggin' clue what I want to do with my life."

"Sure you do." He set the ball back on the table and slumped back in his seat. "I wouldn't expect less from you."

"I'm just looking forward to graduating and getting the hell out of Eastline."

"And then what?"

How had he managed to turn the tables on me again? It was one thing to have these honest—dare I say, intimate—conversations with Morgan or Richard, but how did I know I could trust Brett with my innermost desires? "Going to college and finding the answer to world peace."

"That sounds like something your mother would say." He leaned on the table, his body turned toward mine. "What do you want to do when you get out of college?"

I fought the urge to jump up from the table in an urgent need to refill my glass. Or better yet, help myself to some of my mom's chardonnay. "I've tossed around the idea of going to law school."

"And then what?"

"You said it yourself—I'm good at ball busting. Maybe become a prosecutor."

He nodded. "I can definitely see you doing something like that, especially after reading your blog. You like exposing wrongs."

Once he turned back to the assignment, the muscles in my body finally started to unkink themselves. What was it about him that kept setting me on edge? Kept making me struggle to maintain my boundaries and not let him get closer?

Even though I secretly longed to let him closer?

But I just couldn't. Not now. Maybe not ever.

We both got points for being seniors. And Brett only raised a brow when he saw me mark the line about having the absence of a parent from home. He'd probably guessed that my family was completely dysfunctional.

In the end, we tallied up points. Brett's were higher than mine. I pointed to his total. "I can see you're on your way to the ICU at this rate."

"Yeah," he said glumly. "Time to find ways to reduce my stress."

I looked at the clock. "Football practice should be starting soon."

"True." He closed his laptop, but didn't leave the table. "You want to know something?"

"Depends on what it is."

"It kind of helps having someone to talk to who isn't, you know, caught up in the same little world."

"You mean the highly superficial in-crowd?"

"Or the team. Or—well, yeah." He slid his hands into his

pockets and stretched his legs out under the table. "You're kind of unreasonably harsh at times, but sometimes it's needed, and you do have a different perspective on things."

"Like the fact I'm grounded in reality?"

He shrugged. "Or just the fact you're willing to listen. It's like you're one of the few people I can really be myself around."

And once again, I felt that terrifying warmth in my chest that signaled I might actually care about him. Only this time, it flooded into my arms and made me want to wrap them around him in a comforting hug.

I couldn't afford to be soft and sweet and huggy around him, not if I wanted to maintain my status on the pecking order at school.

He straightened up before I gave into temptation. He put his stuff back into his bag. "I suppose I should get going before school lets out and someone sees my car in your driveway."

"I could always just say you were here looking for Taylor."

That got another of those one-note chuckles from him. "I see you've already thought this through."

"Pretty much."

"So you want to meet back here on Wednesday to finish up the assignment?"

Could I handle another afternoon alone with Brett?

Was there a better alternative?

I didn't see any. "Sure."

"All right, then." He got up and moved to the door, stopping in front of my mom's shrine again. "You know, you look a bit like your mom."

"Is that meant to be a compliment or an insult?"

"Just stating a fact."

Just before he left, I blurted out his name, stopping him. My mouth made a few choked sounds before I finally confessed what had been on my mind since yesterday. "Thanks, you know, for being willing to work with me when whoever drew my name chickened out."

He met my gaze, and something new sparked between us. Yes, we've had moments of anger and flirtation and sexual tension and humor. But this was different, more intense. It was almost like we were connected and were baring parts of our souls, as ridiculous as it sounds.

"It wasn't out of pity," he said softly, his voice with a raw edge I'd never heard before.

"Yeah, I know."

And for once, I truly believed him.

"Dear Justin Wallace, if you're going to cheat on your girlfriend with a girl from another school, don't go to the local Fro-Yo shop and share spoons (and spit) with her. People will notice the lip-locking and take pictures."

The Eastline Spy
February, Freshman Year

Chapter 13

The next morning's handoff was made even sweeter by a large vanilla hazelnut nonfat latte…and a smile from Brett. The tension from the previous morning had vanished, and thankfully, he respected my wish to keep our public interactions at a minimum.

That, of course, didn't extend to health class. He took the seat to my right, just as he had last week, and arched a brow at me, daring me to tell him to get lost.

I didn't.

In truth, he did make the class more bearable.

That was the only reason I permitted him to stay.

The bell rang, and Mr. DePaul stood, double clicking on another PowerPoint presentation. "I can see by the flood of emails in my inbox that most of you have completed your stress inventories, and we have a lot of potentially sick teens in this class. So, now we're going to start a discussion on stress reduction. Today's topic: Physical Ways to Reduce Stress."

"Sex," Brett whispered under his breath.

I rolled my eyes. Just when I was beginning to think highly of him, he did something immature and testosterone-injected like that. "I don't think that's what he meant."

DePaul was droning on about the beneficial aftereffects of exercise such as reduced cortisol levels, increased mental acuity, blah blah blah.

Brett nodded to the slide. "Sex is physical exercise."

"So is running," I countered, ignoring the flush that rose into my cheeks.

"But running isn't as fun."

"Football?"

"Still not as fun."

Would sex be fun with him? "Is there a point to this conversation?"

"Just making an observation. Perhaps you should consider it."

If I didn't know better, I'd think Taylor had blabbed about my virginal status, and he was using it to torment me. "Is this some kind of lame pickup line?"

He sent me a wicked grin that sent shivers straight to the pit of my lower stomach. "What do you think?"

Mr. DePaul interrupted me before I could reply. "Is there something you'd like to share with the class, Ms. Wyndham?"

Part of me wanted to melt under the table in complete mortification. The other part of me wanted to call Brett out. "Brett was just talking about how he could reduce his stress level."

"As excited as you two are to be working on your assignment, please keep your discussions for after class." Then he went back to lecturing.

I closed my eyes and wished I could get up and walk out of class right now.

I didn't need them open to know Brett was leaning closer. His scent grew stronger, and my heart rate spiked as though I was on a treadmill that just increased the incline and speed at the same time. "Your face is red," he whispered.

Who needed exercise when I had Brett nearby? "Shut up."

He retreated, quietly laughing as he did. This round was his. He'd successfully gotten a rise out of me, and that was all he seemed to care about until the end of class. Once the bell rang, he revived the subject. "You really need to find a way to loosen up."

"Or my stress levels will reach yours?"

"At least I know how to handle it."

"Oh yes, I forgot, you have a fuck buddy."

That wiped the grin off of his face.

And just in time for Summer to appear. She glared at me from the doorway.

I grabbed my bag, relieved to be baby-free for the rest of the day, and paused long enough to say to her, "You might want to help Brett unwind."

More than likely, she'd offer him a blow job in the parking lot.

I didn't care. Let the hornball have her.

I had a meeting with Morgan at The Purple Dog.

***

"You okay?" Morgan asked as soon as I arrived.

"Why?" I snapped. I'd taken the bus like I'd always done because parking was a nightmare in the U-District, but even the extra time it took using public transportation hadn't quelled the boiling pot of emotions left over from fourth period.

"Because you seem all on edge about something."

"Brett."

I didn't need to say more. Understanding bloomed in her eyes, and she nodded sympathetically. "Just make it until Friday, Alexis."

"I'm trying."

Gavin swung by our table, diverting Morgan's attention from me. She gave him a smile that lit up her face, but he barely acknowledged it. Instead, he said to me, "Hey, Professor, whatcha going to have?"

"Is it too early for vodka?"

His grin left me wondering if he'd be happy to supply it for me in exchange for something. "Depends."

"Never mind. Just a soda—diet."

"You got it, babe."

Babe? My spine grew hackles, arching in indignation from the derogatory term.

Morgan grabbed my wrist, silently urging me to get my shit together.

It worked long enough to let Gavin get out of ear range. "You seriously like this guy?" I asked.

"Yeah."

"Why?"

"Besides the fact he's hot and in college and has those narrow hips that are just perfect for riding?"

I leaned on the table, massaging my temples. "Why does everything today revolve around sex?"

"It revolves around sex every day—you're just too wrapped up in yourself to notice it." She took a sip of her coffee through a straw and flashed Gavin another million-watt smile when he delivered my can of Diet Coke. "So what did Brett do today?"

"Actually, it started yesterday." Thankfully, Morgan had the patience to wait for me to spill my guts about the meeting at my house before saying anything. "Just when I think he's above most of the boys in our class, he does something completely immature."

"Your problem is just that—he's a boy. You need a man."

"He said I was too uptight and that sex might help me cope with my stress better."

"He's right." She set her cup down and hid behind her copy of Aristotle's *Poetics*.

"Thanks for your support. Gee, and here I thought you were my best friend."

She peered over the top of the book. "I am your best friend, which is why I'm agreeing with him. Sex is fun. You'd probably enjoy it if you gave it a try. You're just too picky."

"I'd like to know I'd be with someone who respected me and my body, thank you."

"All men respect a woman who's comfortable with her sexuality and doesn't just use her body as a bartering chip. You just need to do it and get this whole 'losing your virginity' thing out of your system. Then, once you no longer have that hang-up, the fun can begin."

"I wish it was that easy." In truth, I wished I was more like Morgan when it came to boys and sex. She didn't play games. She didn't suffer from slut-shaming or morning-after regrets. To her, sex was purely physical and nothing more. I was too much of a coward to follow her path. I suspected I'd form some sort of emotional attachment—good or bad—to the first guy I slept with.

Morgan went back to reading, and I started working on this week's blog post. Since sex was still on my mind, I decided to do a piece on the objectification of women in light of the recent locker room videos.

Gavin came by about an hour later, pulling up a chair. "So, what are you working on today?"

Morgan held up her book. "Aristotle."

"A blog post," I replied while I typed.

Gavin peered around my shoulder at my screen. "Feminist?"

"You have a problem with that?"

"Nope." He crossed his arms over the back of the chair. "I think women have a right to do whatever they want, babe."

My shoulders tightened every time he called me that. "Then why do you sound like you're indulging me?"

Morgan hissed my name and sent me another "shut the hell up" look, but Gavin didn't notice.

"Because I think you're going down the wrong path of feminism there. I mean, yeah, women shouldn't be objectified and pointed to and giggled at and all that, but in the same respect, most women want a double standard. They walk around in clothes that highlight their best assets and then smack us guys for noticing them."

"There's a difference between looking and touching."

"Totally, but what you women don't realize is how much power you have over a man. I can't tell you how many of my friends have been completely pussy-whipped by a woman who knows how to use her body."

"So you're saying that we use sex to manipulate men?" I glanced across the table, having heard a variation of this argument from Morgan a hundred times before.

She took my cue and jumped in. "Not all women are like that. Some women just like sex."

"And more power to them for it." Gavin winked at her.

I hoped this little discussion would end with the two of

them hooking up so I wouldn't have to endure his company much longer.

"Besides," he continued, his voice turning slow and seductive, "there's objectification of women as an object of appetite, and then there's the worship of women as an equal partner in mutual desire."

Morgan got lovey-dovey eyes when she heard his line of bullshit. "That's such a profound statement."

I'd heard it before, too. "Where did you read that?"

He cleared his throat and looked away from me. "I came up with it on my own."

"Funny, because my dad published a paper discussing the same thing several years ago. Perhaps you've heard of him—Dr. Grant Wyndham?"

He still refused to meet my gaze. "I got to go back to work." He bolted for the counter, leaving a pissed-off Morgan glaring at me.

"Damn it, Alexis, why do you have to act like such a know-it-all bitch?"

"Because he was totally trying to pass my dad's stuff off as his own."

"But what if he meant it?"

"You mean you actually believe him?"

"Argh, you're impossible." She slammed her book on the table and disappeared down the hall to the bathroom.

Thirty seconds later, Gavin was back at my table. "So Grant Wyndham's your dad?"

"Yes," I replied, not looking up from my keyboard as I continued my rant on sex-crazed assholes.

"I'm a big fan of his work."

"I noticed."

"Perhaps we can hang out sometime and discuss it over

dinner or a drink or something?"

My train of thought slammed on the brakes, and I froze mid-sentence. I lifted my gaze. "Are you asking me out?"

Gavin straightened up from his typical slouch. "Yeah."

"You do realize that Morgan has a serious case of the hots for you and that's a shitty thing for any girl to do to her best friend?"

He nodded.

"And you're asking me out instead of her?"

He nodded again.

"Why?"

"Because you're cooler than her. I mean, she seems nice and all, but she's got some serious baggage, if you know what I mean."

Boy, did I ever. "Since you're a philosophy student, let me give you a little insight about women, especially best friends. We don't go out with guys our best friend is crushing on. It's sort of an unspoken rule. Got it?"

"Yeah, but if she wasn't interested in me?"

I wanted to say fat chance. Thankfully, Morgan's return spared Gavin the reality check he had coming.

"You're brave, coming back here after Alexis was so rude to you," she said, laying her hand on his arm and practically cuddling up to him.

He gave her a half-hug that screamed "just friends" and added some breathing room between them when it ended. "I wanted to let her know how cool I thought her dad was and what an inspiration his writing's been for me."

Oh. My. God. The guy was such a player. And Morgan was stupid enough (or maybe just horny enough) to fall for his crap.

"Yeah, Grant's one of the experts on the philosophy of

love and sex." Morgan coyly bit her bottom lip with the last word, making it very clear what she'd like with Gavin.

I wondered if he had enough decency not to take advantage of her invitation and use her just for a quick screw. Maybe it was because he didn't want to get tangled up in her baggage. He added another step between them. "He's awesome." He jerked his thumb over his shoulder, continuing to backpedal. "I'd love to stay and chat, but I got to work."

"Bye." Morgan gave him a flirtatious little wave, her eyes glued to his butt as he left.

I watched him disappear into the back room before saying, "He's such a douche."

"Alexis!" Morgan snapped her head back to me. "He was just trying to apologize."

"No, he wasn't."

"Then what were you two talking about?"

I debated whether to mention that he was hitting on me. "We were talking about my dad."

She leaned back in her chair and sighed. "I wish we could do a parent swap."

"You want my mom?"

"She's not much different from my mom. Besides, your dad is awesome."

He was—when he wasn't chasing after girls half his age. "I'll agree to a parent swap, but only if you take Taylor."

"Okay, that's the deal breaker." She sat up and opened her copy of *Poetics*. "But please, stop being so hard on him. You're going to scare him away."

And what if I thought that was in her best interest?

But I kept my mouth shut. Gavin was making it clear he wasn't interested in her. Hopefully, Morgan would get the hint soon and move on to someone else.

Confessions of a Queen B*

*"Jared Von Houser, if you're going to call out your ex-girlfriend for
cheating on you by spray painting her name on the side of the school, try
to remember that "slut" only has one T in it. We don't want our school
defiled by spelling errors."*

The Eastline Spy
March, Freshman Year

Chapter 14

I woke up Wednesday morning with an odd swirling of
anticipation in my stomach. By the time I reached school, it
had progressed to a definite variation of queasiness softened
only by the fact Brett had an entourage around him when he
dropped off Junior and didn't have time for any conversation.

When fourth period came around, I was completely on
edge, and I knew why.

I was going to be home alone with Brett in an hour.

Today's lecture was on nonphysical ways to relieve stress—
which hopefully meant Brett wouldn't bring up sex or my need
for it again.

I refused to even look at him for fear it would start another
conversation that would leave me flushed and embarrassed.
And for his part, Brett appeared to be focused on the lecture
and taking notes. No evidence of the heat and tension from

yesterday.

Maybe he did get a blow job from Summer.

The bell rang, and my stomach lurched into my chest.

"So, we're going back to your place?" Brett asked.

Although I doubted he intended it, his question was cloaked with innuendo.

I nodded, focusing on putting my things away and strapping on the baby carrier.

"Good. Then I'll see you in a bit."

My breathing quickened. You'd think we were going back to my place to have some naked playtime, not work on a school project.

Of course, if Brett was right about sex being a great way to relieve stress…

I shook that thought from my head, relieved to see no one was there to witness my mental deterioration. I had enough stress in my life before Brett entered it. This increasing tension between us wasn't helping matters, but it would pass. In three days, our project would be over, and I wouldn't have to worry about being alone with a hot guy who smelled like temptation and made my hormones cloud my better judgment.

Of course, if I cleared the tension between us the old-fashioned way, would that help matters, or hurt them? I mean, yes, there would be less fantasizing about how his lips would feel against mine, where his hands would go, what his skin would taste like…

Snap out of it!

I couldn't go there, no matter how pleasant it seemed in my lust-driven mind, because there would always be that awkward "after" phase. I'd seen it enough times in the hallway on Monday mornings. The hopeful glint in a person's eyes when he or she saw their weekend fling coming toward him or her, followed by that, "um, you're nice and all, but…" conversation. I refused to get caught in that same situation, especially when I knew there was no chance in hell that Brett and I could ever be a "couple."

I needed to cool down the uncomfortable heat that had swarmed my skin from thinking about Brett, so I made a detour to the fro-yo place on the way home. Even though I surveyed the fifteen other flavors available, I always got the same thing. Mocha frozen yogurt with mini dark chocolate chips, brownie bites, and a spoonful of marshmallow cream on top. Maybe one day, I'd try something new, but today, I needed comfort that came from familiarity.

I was standing in line to pay when I overheard a group of guys snickering behind me. I glanced over my shoulder to see Sanchez and several of his teammates gathered around an iPad, their eyes glued to the screen. More juvenile snickers followed, and I rolled my eyes.

Then Sanchez said, "See, I told you guys they were fake."

"I don't care," one of the others replied. "Tits are tits, and that's still an impressive rack."

My annoyance evaporated, leaving behind a trickle of fear. I zeroed in on their conversation, hoping to God this wasn't what I thought it was.

"Oh, look, the little sophomore has to stuff hers," Sanchez said as though he was indulging a toddler. "There's no way she's going to make head cheerleader with those."

My stomach plummeted. They didn't have to name names for me to know who they were talking about. No one talked about my little sister that way.

I grabbed my container of frozen yogurt and marched over to the group of guys. They were too busy enjoying the free peep show that they never saw me coming. I "tripped" and dumped the entire cup of wet frozen yogurt and sticky marshmallow cream over the screen. "Oops!"

Sanchez's face turned a mottled shade of red, his jaw clenched tight. "Why, you—"

One of his teammates held him back, but I didn't care. I didn't fear him. I stood my ground, my glare never wavering from his. "It was an accident," I said innocently. Then I added in a slightly louder voice so the entire fro-yo café could hear, "I'm so sorry I interrupted your porn party."

Sanchez lunged at me again, this time prompting another one of his teammates to restrain him.

I stayed where I was, silently daring him to throw a punch at me in front of everyone. When I filed a police report for assault, I'd have plenty of witnesses.

I held out my napkin. "Can I help you clean up?"

Sanchez's face had gone from red to purple now, the cords on his neck popping out under his skin. "Get the fuck out of my face before I—"

"Dude, chill!" The broadest of the football players moved in front of him, blocking his view of me. "She's not worth getting kicked off the team."

That was interesting to learn. Was Sanchez already in hot water? Definitely something to investigate for my blog later.

But right now, there were more important matters to deal with. I turned and left, my mind still reeling from what I'd overheard. The pervert had posted the videos online again. And this time, he was going to pay.

I was so wrapped up in my plans for vengeance that I'd forgotten all about Brett until I saw the 4Runner sitting in my driveway. He hopped out of his SUV when I drove up. One look at my foul mood, and his smile faded. "What happened to you?"

149

"I don't want to talk about it." More than likely, he already knew about the locker room videos. It seemed the whole football team did.

He moved between me and my front door, stopping me by bracing his hands against my shoulders. "Lexi, talk to me. Tell me what has you so pissed off."

"Like you don't know."

"No, I don't."

I searched his face for any signs of lying, but didn't see any. Maybe he was as innocent as he claimed. I sucked in a deep breath and exhaled, letting some of my anger flow out with the air. "Can we talk about it inside, please?"

"Lead the way."

I was still queasy, but for an entirely different reason now. I'd failed to protect my sister. And that asshole had won—at least for now. But I didn't know if telling Brett about the videos would make things better.

Brett pulled out a chair for me at the table and waited until I sat down before doing the same. "Now, tell me what happened."

"I had a run-in with Sanchez at the fro-yo café." That was common knowledge. Or at least, it would be by morning.

"And?"

"I accidentally tripped and spilled yogurt on his iPad."

Brett crossed his arms. "And why did you do that?"

"It was an accident."

"Nothing about you is an accident."

"Listen, I have things I need to do, so if we can just wrap up this project, I'd appreciate it."

I tried to rise from my chair, but he pushed me back down. "I can't work with you when you're upset, and I can't help you if you won't tell me what's wrong."

"Why do you want to help me? I thought you and Sanchez were best buds."

"We're teammates, but I also know he can be an asshole."

I mirrored Brett's posture, tapping my fingers on my arm as I weighed the consequences of telling him about the video. Finally, I blew a stray strand of hair out of my face and said, "He was watching a naked video of Taylor and some other girls in the locker room."

Brett's expression turned unreadable. "And was this a video she sent to him?"

"Damn it, Brett, I know my little sister can be an idiot at times, but she's not so desperate for attention that she'd stoop to sexting."

"Maybe. Maybe not. I need more information about this video."

My feet twitched, releasing some of the frustrated energy zapping through my veins. I bit my bottom lip, willing Brett to let this subject go so I could take of it myself once we finished our assignment, but in the end, I decided it was better to defend my sister.

"Okay, I'll start from the beginning. Last week, Taylor discovered a video of her and the other cheerleaders on YouTube that had been taken with a hidden camera in the locker room. I went in the next day and found it, left a video message for the perv who'd placed it there to take down the videos, and then threw the camera away. A couple of days later, the videos were gone, and I thought this was over, but then there was this weird post on my blog this weekend and—"

Brett silenced me by placing his hands on my shoulders and giving me a small shake. "Can you show me where the videos were before?"

"Why? So you can get a glimpse of half-naked cheerleaders too?"

"Lexi, please, I'm trying to help you, remember?"

"Fine." I pulled out my laptop and searched through my browser's history until I came to the link. As before, there was a message that the videos had been taken down by the original poster.

Brett took the laptop from me and started typing. "Are you certain that Sanchez was watching videos about your sister and not someone else?"

"Absolutely." How many sophomore cheerleaders used inserts in their bras?

"Let me look into this, then." He gave me the laptop back and pulled out his phone. He typed a quick text message, and less than a minute later, his phone chirped with the reply. He clicked on it and grimaced as the sound of high-pitched giggles poured out from his speakers.

"Sanchez sent you the link?" I asked dryly, timing how long Brett watched the video.

"Yeah." A few more seconds passed before he stopped it and set his phone on the table. He rubbed his eyes as though he wanted erase those images from his mind. "I've seen enough. You're right about the video."

"And now you know why Sanchez's iPad was attacked by my cup of mocha frozen yogurt."

The corner of his mouth quirked up. "Mocha, huh?"

"My favorite flavor," I said with a sigh. "It was sacrificed for a good cause, though."

"It may have ended Sanchez's viewing pleasure, but that video's still out there. The guy just reposted it under a different alias."

"Is there any way we can get it taken down?"

Now it was his turn to hesitate. "Maybe."

"Meaning?"

"People can post stuff like this on YouTube."

"Yes, but this video was made without the consent of those involved." I pressed my finger against his phone, deciding to try a new angle. "What if it was one of your sisters in the locker room?"

His lips thinned, and a hint of anger simmered in his eyes. "I'd go after the bastard myself."

"Well, it's my sister in those videos, and now you know why I want to go after him."

Brett slid my finger off his phone and picked it up again. "So this is all about protecting Taylor, huh?"

"Yeah. I mean, we're nothing alike, but in the end, she's still my little sister. You understand, right?"

"Absolutely." He touched his screen, and the voices filled the airwaves again.

I snatched the phone out of his hands. "If you understand, then why are you going back for seconds?"

"Because I noticed something," he replied, taking his phone back.

"What?"

He paused the video and showed me the image on the screen. Taylor stood in the middle in her bra and panties, a bright pink ribbon around her ponytail. "Is that the same ribbon she was wearing yesterday?"

All the blood rushed from my head. Not only had the pervert gone back to posting videos of my sister, he'd replaced the camera. That comment on my blog wasn't a warning. It was a challenge. The asshole had just given me the middle finger by going back in there and recording my sister undressing again. I jumped up from my chair, my feet unsteady.

A pair of warm hands kept me from tripping for real this time. "Hold on, Lexi. Think about this before you rush into it and make things worse."

"I have to find that camera and take it down now."

"Fine, but I'm coming with you."

The blood made its way back up to my brain in less than a second. "Like hell you are. The camera's in the girls' locker room. You aren't allowed in there."

"I'll take my chances if it means I can help you uncover who's behind this."

I wobbled again, this time out of shock. "You're willing to risk getting in trouble to help me?"

"Yes."

I wanted to ask him why, but fear held my tongue. I didn't want to know it was because he felt sorry for me because I'd done a completely shitty job the last time. Instead, I took advantage of his hands on my shoulders, allowing myself a moment to lean on him.

But before my head could reach his shoulder, Junior started wailing.

"Shit!" I said under my breath, jerking back from Brett. "I'm beginning to hate that damn doll."

"I've got it." He released me and immediately began the pretend diaper change. "You go ahead and make sure the locker room is empty. I'll be along in a few minutes."

"What about the doll?"

"I'll drop it off with my mom. She won't mind watching it for an hour or so."

"I'll pick him up from her once we find the camera."

"No worries." Junior was quiet now, but Brett was already gathering the bottle and carrier. "You know where I live."

I backed away, still watching him. "Thanks."

"No need to thank me. Like you said, I have younger sisters." He followed me to the front door, adding, "It's the right thing to do."

As I drove off, I half-expected to see some kind of superhero cape flutter around Brett's shoulders.

"It seems the school locker rooms have gone co-ed, judging by the frequency Scott Davis and Jenny McMichael have been spotted visiting them in between classes."

The Eastline Spy
June, Junior Year

Chapter 15

I got to school just as classes were changing. It was easy to melt into the crowds of students on campus and make my way to the locker room with the poor souls—mostly freshmen—who had P.E. for sixth period. I hid in one of the bathroom stalls while they changed and filtered out in groups of twos and threes. Once it was silent again, I ventured out and checked the premises.

It was empty.

I cracked open the door to find Brett waiting beside it. "All clear?"

"All clear." I opened it further and looked around to make sure no one was watching as he slipped in.

He stood a few feet inside like he was afraid to go any further. "So this is what the girls' locker room looks like."

"It's nothing special." I brushed past him, scanning the tops of the lockers for the new camera.

"It smells better."

I remembered the Axe body wash–scented cloud that had billowed out of the boys' locker room Friday night. "It didn't smell too bad in yours after the game."

"That's because we were all getting clean to go out and celebrate. You should've smelled it before the showers."

"I'll pass." I walked down the next row of lockers, but still couldn't find the camera.

Brett was right behind me. "Any idea where the video was shot from?"

"You're the one with the link."

He pulled out his phone and handed it to me to open the link. Perhaps he had seen enough of Summer's enhanced cleavage.

I started the video and moved around the locker room until I found the same vantage point. "It's somewhere around here."

He took his phone back, turning off the video as he slid it back into his pocket. "Then let's start looking."

Unlike last time, there was no big desktop camera sitting on top for me to grab and dispose of. Brett and I both looked along the row of lockers and found nothing.

"I was afraid of this," he muttered. "Time to get technical."

He pulled another device out of his pocket. It was about the size of his phone, but the screen was smaller. A small knob dominated the space below the screen.

"What's that do?"

"It picks up wireless signals."

"And how will that help us find the camera?"

"Unless the person behind the videos is hiding in a locker with a handheld camera the entire time, the images are being sent through a wireless connection." He pulled a small LED flashlight out of his other pocket. "Here, take this and shine it into the slats of the lockers."

I did as he told me to do while he slowly scanned the lockers with his device, his eyes focused on the screen. I found nothing.

He stopped about halfway down the line of lockers, his brows drawn together. "Come back over here and take another look. There's a strong signal coming from this one."

The locker in front of him had a dark blue padlock on it. I scanned the slats. The light flashed on something in the upper left hand corner. I repeated the movement and got the same result. "Something's there."

Brett took the flashlight from me and saw the same the thing. "I think we might've found our camera."

He handed me the flashlight again and reached into the cargo pocket of his shorts. This time, he pulled out a bolt cutter.

"Let me guess—you're a Boy Scout, too?"

"Nope, but it never hurts to be prepared." He started working on the padlock. "I'm just glad I stopped by my house on the way over here."

A couple of minutes later, the lock yielded and fell to the ground with a loud clang. I opened the locker and found an old iPod taped to the door with a set of wires coming from the charging port and a wireless router. "Bingo."

Brett seemed more interested in the wires than the actual camera. "This is pretty clever. Whoever put it there put a lot of thought into making sure the iPod had plenty of power, and it looks like he was remotely enabling the recordings through FaceTime."

"I don't care—I just want it gone." I tugged at the last of the duct tape holding it up and ripped the device off the door.

Then I pressed the red circle with the phone icon. "Time to end this call."

Brett held out his hand, still studying the snarl of wires in the locker. "Let me see it."

"Fine." I handed it over to him and waited for him to finish investigating the setup.

Voices filtered in from the windows outside, slowly growing louder. My gut tensed. Someone was coming this way.

I jostled Brett's shoulder, but he waved me away. "In a minute."

The entrance of the locker room creaked open. My pulse jumped into overdrive. We were seconds away from getting caught. I searched for a place to hide. Someone would see our feet if we hid in a bathroom stall (unless we decided to stand on the toilet seats, but *ick*!). The way out was blocked.

But by some small blessing, the door to the janitor's closet wasn't fully closed. Which meant it wasn't locked like usual.

I grabbed Brett by his shirt and dragged him over to it as the front door of the locker room banged open. A deep male voice I immediately recognized as Principal Lee's echoed off tile walls. "Someone said they saw a guy sneaking in here."

Shit! That blog post I'd written last year about students cutting class to make out in the locker rooms was coming back to haunt me.

I pushed Brett into the janitor closet and pulled the door closed behind us as quietly as I dared. If we made any noise, I couldn't hear it over the pounding of my heart and the continual string of four-letter words repeating through my head.

"I'll take a look around," a woman said. Coach Dittmer.

The closet was pitch black, but I had no trouble finding Brett's mouth. I placed my fingers over his lips to remind him to keep quiet.

I'd been terrified about Brett getting caught in the locker room, but as he wrapped his arm around my waist, I quickly came to realize I should've been more afraid of getting caught *with* him.

My heart continued to race, but for a very different reason. We were pressed together in the small space, his arm holding me close to him. I breathed him in with every stunted breath I took, acutely aware of how close he was and how that affected me.

He covered my hand, still on his lips, and placed a single kiss on my fingertips.

A jolt coursed down my spine.

Outside the closet, I continued to hear the voices, but I didn't know what was more dangerous—bolting from the closet and getting caught by the principal, or staying here with Brett.

In the darkness, I couldn't see his face, so I had no idea of his motives. For all I knew, this was just a continuation of his successful attempt to get a rise out of me by talking about sex. Only now, his lips were doing the talking in an unexpected way.

He took my hand and placed it on his chest, still holding me against him. His heart was drumming through his chest at the same breakneck speed as mine.

I held my breath, wondering what he was planning on doing next.

I didn't have to wait long. His fingers traveled up my arm to my shoulder, leaving a trail of heat in their wake. And yet despite the warmth that rushed through my veins, I shivered and pressed my body even closer to his.

His fingers continue up my neck, finally stopping under my

chin. He tilted it up.

And somehow through the darkness, his lips found mine.

Oh, holy shit, I was kissing Brett Pederson!

Or to be more precise, he was kissing me.

It was a simple kiss, as far as kisses go. No tongue. No biting. Just the firm pressure of his lips moving against mine. Time seemed to stop, so I had no idea how long we stayed there. I only knew that when he tried to end it, my body protested.

I slipped my arm over his shoulder, threading my fingers through his short hair.

He froze, sucking in a breath and holding it.

Then I did the unthinkable. I pulled his head toward me and kissed him back.

Only my kiss was nowhere near as polite and restrained as his was. If I was going to slip into a moment of temporary insanity and make out with the quarterback, I was going to go all out. I pushed him back against the wall, my lips still glued to his. His grip loosened on me, and for a split second, I wondered if I had taken things too far. But when his hands reached under my shirt, I grew bolder, more aggressive.

My tongue traced the seam of his mouth, silently begging permission to enter. He wasted no time opening up to me and taking my breath away with his own skills. We kissed like two starving souls who couldn't get enough of each other, our tongues clashing as much now as they had with our verbal sparring over the last week and a half.

Only, I had to admit, I was enjoying this way, way more.

My hands roamed his hard body, from his broad shoulders to his firm ass that fit beautifully in my palms. He reciprocated, his hands kneading my behind while we continued to kiss like a couple heading straight for the bedroom instead of two students hiding from the principal.

I should've been shocked by my brazen actions. I should've been horrified that I enjoyed making out with Brett as much as I did. I should've remembered why we were hiding in a dark janitor's closet that smelled faintly of bleach in the first place. But any mental capacity I had flew out the door the moment Brett pressed my fingers against his mouth and started this dangerous chain reaction.

My breath was coming hot and heavy, and my hips started rocking in a seductive tempo that matched the movements of our tongues. A soft moan rose from one of our throats—I couldn't tell whose. One of Brett's hands got tangled up in my hair, massaging my scalp and encouraging me to continue.

Trust me, I had no intention of stopping at the moment. I only wanted to take things further. I dragged my hands over his shoulders, searching for the buttons of his shirt. One by one, I unfastened them until I could freely explore the planes of his chest.

He followed my lead, his hands under my T-shirt, slowly tugging it up and forcing me to end our game of tonsil hockey long enough to pull it over my head.

And I was so glad he did. My bra stayed on, but otherwise, I was chest to chest with him. The heat of his bare skin against mine awakened a new level of desire, of longing, of sensations I never dreamed possible. I'd always wondered how Morgan could easily hook up with guys she hardly knew for a few rounds of wild, hot sex. Now I knew. Brett and I were already half-naked, and I didn't want to stop. It felt so wicked, so indulgent.

So damn good.

Brett had been right—sex was definitely a stress reliever. My cares were as far away as they could possibly be, and we still had our pants on.

And speaking of pants, the ever-hardening ridge beneath his shorts let me know that he was as turned on as I was—maybe more. Based on the way he was grinding against me, he wasn't making any effort to hide his attraction, either.

The dynamics slowly shifted. Now, he was the one calling the shots. He was the one pressing me against the cold metal door that contrasted with the burning flesh of our bodies. He was the one exploring my curves with his hands, cupping my ass first and then working his way up to my breasts. Each touch awakened a new level of wantonness in me. Each stroke left me begging for more.

My lungs were working overtime to the point where I grew dizzy, forcing me to tear my lips away from his long enough to breathe.

That didn't stop Brett, though. His mouth moved to my ear. "Damn it, Lexi," he groaned.

I couldn't find the words. I just held on to him since he was the only thing keeping me from sliding onto the floor at the moment.

He reached behind me, trying to unhook my bra while my shoulder was in his mouth. The series of nips and gentle sucks along that area of skin nearly turned me to Jell-O and erased any outrage I thought I might have felt about a guy trying to get past second base. At this point, I was praying for a home run.

I wanted Brett Pederson more than I had wanted any other guy in my life, and at that moment, I was willing to do whatever he wanted as long as he continued kissing me.

A loud bang shook the walls, and Brett's head snapped up from my neck.

The heat from our blissful make-out session vanished, and

the cold reality of our situation crashed into me like an eighteen-wheeler.

I was half naked in a janitorial closet with the one guy I had no chance of ever having a serious relationship with. The one guy who was part of a crowd that stood for everything I looked down on.

The one guy who was so wrong and yet was dangerously right.

"Shit!" I shoved him away and crossed my arms over my chest.

"Lexi, what—"

"Oh my God," I whispered as I blindly searched for my T-shirt. My legs quivered, threatening to give out on me as the blood rushed back to my head. What had I just done?

My shirt was hanging from the mop handle. I yanked it over my head and wasted no time feeling for the doorknob. I didn't care if we got caught and accused of smoking pot any more. I was already one step away from the loony bin, and suspension would probably be my saving grace. I just needed to get away from Brett before he touched me, before he kissed me again and took me back to brink of insanity.

I stumbled out into the locker room, pressing my hands against my flaming hot cheeks while I gulped in the cool air. Coach Dittmer and the principal were gone. No one was there to witness Brett and me coming out of the closet with our rumpled clothes and wild hair.

A hand landed on my shoulder, and I jumped. "Lexi, tell me what's wrong."

What was wrong was that I was friggin' enjoying making out with him way more than I should. But I kept that to myself. I wasn't ready to admit that to anyone. Besides, Brett already had plenty of dirt on me after what just had happened.

My voice shook as I said, "I've gotta go."

I ran for the door, tripping over benches and bumping into lockers along the way. I'd handle the bruises later. I just needed to get as far away from Brett as I could.

I didn't stop running until I got to my car. As I put on my seatbelt, I realized I'd put my shirt on backward and inside out, but I could fix that as soon as I got home. I drove away, waiting for the guilt and shame that were undoubtedly coming my way for losing control of myself like that, but they never came. My mind was the only part of me that was still going "shit, shit, shit," and that was only because I was still in shock that:

A) Brett Pederson had kissed me
B) I had kissed him back
C) I really, really, REALLY enjoyed it.

Yeah, definitely time to voluntarily commit myself.

I got home and dashed up to my room to change. When I removed my shirt, I noticed that it smelled like Brett. Any rational person would've thrown it in the laundry and walked away, but I still wasn't thinking rationally yet. I was too busy remembering how good it felt in his arms. I lay down on my bed and cuddled with the balled-up T-shirt, holding it close to my nose and breathing it in as I replayed those crazy, but oh so pleasurable, moments in the closet with Brett over and over again.

Tomorrow was going to suck.

But I'd deal with it tomorrow.

"After last year's police raid of the campus, I know some members of the student body have been missing their daily dose of Adderall or Percocet. But never fear. There's a new candy man on campus, so if you need any prescription drugs that your doctor won't give you, just look for the man with the orange bandana in the parking lot after school."

The Eastline Spy
November, Sophomore Year

Chapter 16

The house was dark and quiet when I opened my eyes. The red lights from my alarm clock read 11:56 p.m. I had no idea when I'd fallen asleep, but I'd wasted the rest of the afternoon moping in bed. Now, the rumbling in my stomach from missing both lunch and dinner surpassed the turmoil in my head and heart.

I changed into my PJs before heading downstairs to grab something from the fridge so I could focus on getting my homework done. I did a double take when I stumbled upon my mom sitting at the island. "Didn't expect to find you here," I mumbled as I passed her.

"Just unwinding from a long day," she replied before taking a substantial sip from her wineglass and going back to something on her iPad. "What are you doing up?"

This was where I could've lied and claimed to be ill and not gone to school for, say, the rest of the year. That was the safest way to avoid any more contact with Brett. Instead, I grabbed an apple and leaned on the island's counter across from her. "Boy trouble."

That got her attention. Possibly from the fact she'd probably never dreamed I'd ever have boy trouble since I'd never had a serious boyfriend. She actually turned her iPad off and put it aside. "Care to talk about it?"

As awkward a conversation as this could be, it was better than the alternatives. I could never admit what I'd done to Richard and Morgan—they'd rip me to shreds. And my dad…well, I already had a good idea what he'd say.

I pulled a stool over, thankful to have the slab of cold granite between us while I figured out where to start. "There's a guy at school I shouldn't like, that I shouldn't be attracted to, but I kind of am."

Mom nodded, pouring a new glass of wine and sliding it toward me. "Why?"

Way to wrench a drunken confession from me, Mom.

"Why what?" I sniffed the wine. It smelled faintly of peaches. Tasted like it, too.

"Why do you think you shouldn't like him? Is he a criminal? Does he do drugs?"

The image of clean-cut Brett lighting up a joint flickered across my mind, and I choked on the wine. I coughed a few times between giggles before catching my breath again. "No."

"Then what do you find objectionable about him?"

"He's…" Somehow, I didn't think my mom would remember the high school social hierarchy, and even if she did, it would be from her perspective as a former beauty queen. "He's more Taylor's type, I guess you'd say."

Mom merely nodded, drinking her wine and waiting for me to continue.

"Or at least I thought he was," I added, remembering how he turned all geek when he saw the elaborate setup around the camera. "He might actually be kind of smart—you know, more than just a dumb jock."

"That doesn't sound like something that should bother you. You tend to like intelligent people."

"And if we were just talking or whatever, that wouldn't be a problem. But this afternoon, I—we—crossed a line, and I'm more confused than ever."

"And by 'crossed a line,' " Mom repeated, using air quotes for added emphasis, "do you mean you two got physical?"

And then things officially turned awkward. I finished off the glass of wine, hoping it would ease my embarrassment. "Just a little."

Mom set her glass aside and studied me, not paying attention to how much I squirmed on my barstool as she did.

"I would usually go to Dad with something like this," I began, but stopped when I saw the hurt in her eyes. "Not that I wouldn't want to come to you, but you've been so busy lately, and—"

She swallowed, the regret still lingering in the corners of her eyes.

"Besides, I know what Dad would say if brought this to him. He'd say—"

"Fuck him," Mom finished for me, although I had no idea if it was directed toward Dad or was meant to indicate what Dad would say in this situation. "There's a reason why your father is a professor on the philosophy of sex—he's constantly thinking with his dick."

And we just added another layer of awkward. At this rate, I wouldn't have anyone I'd feel safe talking to. Time to set up that anonymous Twitter account to vent my soul in a hundred and forty characters or less. My first tweet: "Hormones suck, but damn, they feel good at times."

"Did you have sex with him?" Mom asked in her doctor

voice.

"No."

"But you got physically involved with him?" She did a visual inspection of me as though she were looking for my scarlet letter. "Did he hit you?"

"No," I said again, this time with more frustration in my voice as I set my empty wineglass on the counter with a bit more force than necessary. "We just started making out like the two horny teenagers we are. And when I finally came to my senses, I realized it had been a mistake, so I came home. End of story."

"But it's not the end of the story if it's still bothering you." She refilled my glass and hers with the rest of the bottle. I could count on one hand the number of times I'd had alcohol with my mom, and I would still have fingers to spare after tonight. "Let's go back to the beginning of our conversation. You said you shouldn't like him, but you do, right?"

I ran my finger along the rim of the wineglass, not knowing how to answer the question. "Maybe."

"You found him intelligent." My mom held up one finger. "He's not into drugs." Another finger. "He doesn't hit you." Another finger. "And it sounds like he's a good kisser." A fourth finger. "Am I missing anything else?"

"You forgot that he's the starting quarterback of the football team, extremely hot, and way out of my league." I held up three fingers, all representing the three strikes against him.

"Those points make him sound even better. Anything else about Mr. Wonderful?"

I chewed my bottom lip. "He wants to help me solve my problems, and he makes great blueberry pancakes."

Mom placed her hand on my forehead. "Are you sure you're well? Because if you're having doubts about a guy like that, then you're either crazy or there's something you're not telling me."

I pushed her hand away. "The only crazy going on here is why he'd be into me. This is the type of guy who goes for head cheerleaders, not the meanest girl in school."

"And he sounds like he's into you if he's cooking you breakfast." She started to take another sip of wine, but paused with the glass millimeters from her lip and eyed me over the rim. "You're on the pill, right?"

"Mom!" My cheeks were burning now, and not from the wine. "Making out does not equate sex."

"Yeah, but if you let things get out of control again…"

"Then that solves it." I stood up, pushing my wineglass back. "I won't let things get out of control again. As long as I don't allow myself to be in a situation where I'm alone with Brett, then we'll be forced to keep our hands to ourselves." And our lips.

Damn it.

"Sounds like a solid plan." Mom went back to finishing her wine as I walked away, content that this conversation was over. "By the way, Alexis, you might want to wear something that covers up that hickey on your shoulder for the next few days."

My stomach dropped, and I raced to the downstairs bathroom. Under the glaring lights above the mirror, I saw the telltale purple bruise where my shoulder met my neck.

The same place where Brett had done wonderfully naughty things with his teeth, tongue, and lips.

Now on display for everyone to see.

I was so screwed.

"OK, I get it. You're taking school violence very seriously based on the way you closed down the school for three days after someone anonymously threatened to pick off certain students with a sniper rifle. But maybe if you'd done something about the bullying and hazing that happens every day in the hallways, that anonymous student wouldn't have felt the need to resort to his threat."

The Eastline Spy
January, Junior Year

Chapter 17

Brett wasn't at my locker when I arrived at school the next morning.

I told myself that I shouldn't be surprised. I mean, I was the one who ran off and left him in the girls' locker room yesterday afternoon. Rejection like that would wound any guy's pride.

Then my throat tightened. What if he'd been caught and suspended? What if he'd gotten in trouble because of me?

The guilt I'd been expecting since yesterday finally rammed into me, but not because of those few intense moments in the janitor's closet.

I was actually beginning to care about Brett.

Yeah, I was in serious shit. I pulled out my phone and

started texting him, asking him where he was.

A minute later, my phone vibrated with the reply.

Overslept. See you in 4ᵗʰ period.

My worry whooshed out in a sigh of relief. Of course, that still meant I had to deal with him then. But it gave me more time to practice the "yesterday was a one-time fluke" speech. By the time fourth period came around, I had it memorized. I was going to politely tell him that he'd taken advantage of our situation, and I'd responded with poor judgment, but now after I'd had time to digest my actions, I wanted to let him know it would never happen again.

The words vanished from my mind the second he sat down next to me. In their place came a whiny little bitch of a voice clamoring for more one-on-one time with Brett. *Please, please, please, please!*

I moved to the chair at the opposite end of the table before I gave into it.

He looked at the empty chair between us and then at me before placing the doll in the spot. Dark circles lined his eyes, making his lashes seem thicker than normal. Fatigue sagged around the corners of his mouth. "You forgot to pick up the doll yesterday," he said.

"Shit!" I'd been so completely absorbed in my own little crisis that I'd forgotten about our assignment. "It didn't keep you up all night, did it?"

He shook his head.

"I'll take the doll for the rest of the project," I offered, hoping to make it up to him.

"Fine." He turned to the front of the class as the bell rang, ending our conversation.

Or so I thought.

About three minutes into class, a message popped up on

my laptop screen.

We need to talk about yesterday.

My breath hitched, but that did nothing to slow my frantic heart. I searched the room, looking for the sender before meeting Brett's eyes. They flickered once to my screen and then back to Mr. DePaul.

I watched Brett the entire time as I typed, *No, we don't.*

The message popped up on his screen. His frown deepened. *Why?*

How are you sending me messages on my laptop?

You didn't answer my question.

Did you hack my computer? Put some virus on it?

The corner of his mouth reversed its downward trend and curled up into a half-smile. *I'm just using your school email address to message you, Lexi. Calm down. Anyone in the school network can do it.*

Don't call me Lexi! I paused, remembering some hoopla last year about the school cracking down on messaging programs during class after I'd posted screenshots on my blog of the inappropriate conversations that were occurring. *I thought the school banned this, BTW.*

His grin widened to capture a hint of recklessness, and I caught a glimpse of yet another facet of Brett Pederson—the one who didn't mind breaking a few rules here and there. It fit the same guy who didn't mind making out with random girls in janitors' closets.

Can we meet back at your place after class? he asked.

Rule number one—thou shall not be alone with Brett Pederson. My damp fingertips left marks on my keyboard as I typed, *Sorry—have plans.*

We have a project to finish.

Shit! *I'll take care of your half for you,* I replied. Anything to keep me from having to be alone with him again.

He shook his head. *No, I want my A, too.*

He clicked a few things on his laptop, and an email appeared in my inbox. I opened it and read what he'd done already for his part of the project.

So we really don't need to work together anymore? An ache formed in my chest as I typed that. Once again, my hormones were at war with my common sense.

Minutes ticked by before Brett started his reply. *Only if you don't want to.*

I swallowed—hard—and struggled with the emotions swirling inside me. *It has to be this way.*

Why?

I curled my fingers into my palms, not trusting them to convey my thoughts accurately. I needed the power of my voice and my body to express them, not a blinking cursor on my screen.

Off in the distance, Mr. DePaul droned on and on about something, but my attention remained on the three letters on my screen. I was going to fail health class because Brett Pederson kept distracting me from the material that would be on the final—I knew it.

Time to end this. I took a deep breath and typed, *It's complicated.*

No shit.

Glad to know I wasn't the only one whose stomach was tied in knots after yesterday. *Please, can we pretend yesterday never happened?*

The hickey on my shoulder proved otherwise, but I could always turn to wishful thinking instead of actually dealing with fallout in a mature manner.

Another stretch of silence passed, and I wondered if Brett

had decided it was better to listen to Mr. DePaul's lecture than me. Then, in the waning seconds of class, he wrote, *If that's what you want.*

The bell rang, and he snapped his laptop shut, bolting for the door faster than Sanchez did.

I stared at his words while everyone else filed out of class. Was that really what I wanted?

And even if it was, what could I do about it?

***

I went home and moped. Not even the pint of mocha frozen yogurt I picked up on the way home could cheer me up. Hours later, the half-eaten remains sat in the cup on my desk like muddy soup.

Mom was working late (again), and Taylor was in her room on the phone with one of her friends discussing how to do her hair for the game tomorrow. I was staring at the screen and the almost finished blog post that I'd started earlier this week. It was due to go live at midnight. I'd laid out my arguments. I'd stated why it was wrong to treat women that way. I'd even used the videos as an example.

And yet, it felt incomplete.

I wanted to nail the son of a bitch behind the videos, but I didn't have a name. I didn't even know if the videos had been removed yet. But I wanted justice.

Forget justice. I wanted to publicly humiliate the person behind them after what he'd done to Taylor. After all, what good was being the biggest bitch in school if I couldn't keep people in line?

My phone rang while I was reviewing my editorial one more time, and I picked it up without checking the number.

"Lexi, can you come over for a few minutes?" Brett's voice asked from the other side.

My blood turned to ice, followed by a quick thaw from the rush of heat that followed. "Why?"

"Because I need to show you something."

I licked my lips. Could I trust myself around him, or would I lose control all over again? "Can't you tell me over the phone?"

"No, I need to show you now." He paused and added in a softer tone, "Please."

I thought about it for several beats. He was inviting me to come over to his house, which was crawling with people. It would be safe. More than likely, I would end up braiding Bitsy's hair again. I could handle this. "Okay, I'll be there in a few minutes, but I'll have to bring Junior."

"That's fine. See you in a few." He hung up.

I strapped the carrier to my chest, noting with some pleasure that I wouldn't need it after tomorrow. This was offset by the fact I probably wouldn't be seeing Brett at my locker every morning for the handoff, either. I told myself that should make me happy, too, but it left me empty instead.

It took me less than ten minutes to walk to his house. Once again, Sarah answered the door. "Brett's upstairs in his room," she said, pointing up the staircase. "Last door on the right."

My spit dried up. It was one thing to come to his house with his sisters and parents all around.

But stepping into the secret sanctuary of his room? That simmered with danger.

And intrigue, because as far as I knew, no girl in Eastline High School had been invited up there.

It was curiosity (and knowing I'd have something else over Summer Hoyt) that propelled my feet up the stairs and to the last door on the right. I knocked and waited.

Brett opened the door, grabbed me by the wrist, and

yanked me inside. The door slammed behind us.

Can I say I was a little disappointed when he didn't drag me to bed?

The disappointment quickly wore off as I looked around. Posters lined the walls, but instead of NFL heroes, they were of *Star Wars, Star Trek,* and *Doctor Who.* A bookshelf in the corner contained the expected athletic trophies, but it also housed a Lego version of the Millennium Falcon under a glass cube. And scattered across the room with recent issues of *Sports Illustrated* were back issues of *Circuit Cellular* and other computer magazines, as well as thick fantasy tomes that qualified as weapons in some countries. And in the center of one wall was a computer workstation that would make most Microsofties drool.

My jaw dropped.

Underneath the veneer of Mr. Quarterback, Brett Pederson was a closet geek.

"Sorry, but I didn't want one of the twins trying to sneak in behind you." He cleared a place on his bed for me. "Have a seat."

I raised a brow, remaining remarkably cool considering the circumstances. "I'm not here to finish what we started yesterday."

That wicked gleam flashed in his eyes, followed by a dull seriousness. "Just give me a minute, please." He backed me onto the mattress and retreated to the desk.

So much for making out again.

At least I wouldn't have any fresh hickeys to cover up.

Brett typed away at his computer, his back to me. "First off, I found a way to take down the videos and replace them with this."

A video of two kittens wrestling filled the screen of one of his monitors. My lips twitched. "A definite improvement over seeing Summer's fake boobs."

Brett cleared his throat, a line of red rising into his cheeks. He continued typing. "Second, I think I may have found the person behind the videos."

I jumped to my feet and stood behind him. "Who is it?"

Brett leaned back in his chair, cracked his knuckles, and spun around to face me. A sly grin formed on his lips. "If I told you that information…"

"You'd have to kill me?" I finished, hand on my hip. I doubt I looked the least bit threatening with the damn doll strapped to my chest, but at least it conveyed a hands-off vibe. "Seriously, Brett, I didn't come over here to play games. I have a blog post due by midnight, and if I can crack this scandal open in the process and make this guy pay for what he's done, then I want to do it."

"I understand you wanting revenge, Lexi—if it involved one of my own sisters, I'd feel the same way, but I want to make sure you understand everything before you act without thinking."

"Are you saying I'm impulsive?"

His gaze fell on my lips. "Well, there was yesterday…"

I rolled my eyes and plopped back on the edge of his bed. "Can we please not bring that up?"

"Why?"

"Why do you keep asking why, Brett? It happened, okay? Call it a moment of temporary insanity. I didn't intend for it to happen, but it did. And now you're never going to let me live it down, are you?"

He laced his fingers together like some James Bond villain who enjoyed torturing 007 and seeing if he could break the secret agent. "What happened, happened."

"And if I remember correctly, you instigated it."

His brows rose in mock innocence. "Me?"

"Yes, you. You're the one who kissed me first."

"You were the one who pushed me into the closet."

"Because I was trying to keep you from getting caught by Principal Lee and Coach Dittmer."

His folded hands shielded his mouth, hiding the most expressive part of his face. Had he been so distracted by the wiring of the camera that he didn't hear them? At last, he said in a soft voice, "Maybe so, but you were the one who kissed me back."

My skin itched from the thousands of little prickles of sweat that broke out all over my body. Denying what happened would get me nowhere. It was time to own up to the mistake. "Yeah, I did."

His gaze locked with mine, his mouth still hidden behind his hands and making it harder for me to read his emotions.

My defenses were chattering under that stare, from the intense emotions glowing from his dark eyes, from the way they narrowed like a predator picking apart his prey. I'd never backed down from a challenge—it was one of the ways I'd won my Queen B status—but this time, I had to look away. I focused on the frayed edge of one of the carrier's straps and asked, "So why did you kiss me?"

I dared to look up through my lashes when he didn't answer right away. He hadn't moved, but something had changed in his demeanor. Gone was the cocky predator. In his place sat a guy who looked as awkward and confused as I felt.

"Temporary insanity," he said in a voice so raw it choked my heart.

He turned back to the computer and started typing again. "Between the post on your blog and the clips on YouTube, I was able to track down the ISP address of the original poster."

"English, please." My legs had the steadiness of rubber bands when I stood to approach the desk. I'd survived the discussion, but I'd taken a beating to my soul for it. Thank God I had something else to focus my attention on instead of licking my wounds.

"I was able to get information on where the videos were posted and who posted them. And you were right. They are the same person." A few taps and clicks later, a name appeared on the screen. "Here's your locker room spy."

I squinted at the unfamiliar name. "Adam Kozlovsky. Who is he?"

"I'm not surprised that you don't know who he is. Maybe this will help." A few more clicks, and the image of an Eastline High student ID popped up on the screen.

The graduation year indicated he was a sophomore, but his face was just one of the hundreds that blurred together in the hallways every day. He wore an Eastline baseball cap, but there was nothing athletic about his physique. Zits covered his pudgy cheeks, and thick dark curls peeked out from under the cap. His blank expression showed total disengagement with the photographer.

A new window opened up. "Here's his schedule, if you want to confront him."

I took a step back. "How did you get this information?"

Brett did his best Dr. Horrible impression, ending with the same uneasy wannabe evil laugh. "It's not that hard to hack into the school's system, Alexis."

" 'Hack'? As in illegally gaining access?"

"It's only illegal if you get caught." He twisted from side to side in his chair. "It's not like I'm changing grades or class rank, Miss Potential Valedictorian."

"There's nothing 'potential' about that, Football Boy." Then I caught the threat behind his words. "Wait a minute—have you been spying on my records?"

He just grinned.

"Two can play at this game, you know. I still have that picture."

"I know." He tilted his head toward me. "In this case, I'm enjoying the game."

He was probably the only person in the school who had enough balls to play it. Everyone else preferred to avoid me than meet me head on.

I memorized Adam's schedule, but it wasn't enough. "Can you send me a copy of his ID?"

"Why?"

"Do you have to ask that all the time? It pisses me off."

"I know."

"And let me guess—you enjoy pissing me off?"

"Yep," he said with a self-satisfied smirk.

"Why?"

His eyes traveled from my head to my toes and back again before he stood up from his chair. He closed the space between us, cornering me between his bed and his bookcase.

My lungs burned as I tried to fight the ever-increasing drive to breathe. If I gave into it, he'd see how breathless I became when he was near me, how hard I worked to suppress my attraction to him, how much I craved a repeat of yesterday afternoon.

He unhooked the baby carrier from around me and tossed it and the doll onto his mattress. My last layer of defense had been stripped away, and the heat from his body penetrated mine. "I'm not really pissing you off, you know."

I plastered my back against the wall, pinning my eager

hands behind me to keep from wrapping them around his neck. My bottom lip trembled as I said, "Wanna bet?"

He halted, keeping a few inches of air between us. "You're not pissed off, Lexi. I've seen you angry, and this is not it."

"Then what am I feeling, Mr. Know-It-All?"

"Flustered." He drawled the word out in a low, rumbling whisper.

A shiver raced down my spine. My arms shuddered, and my chest rose and fell like I'd just come from gym class. "Flustered?"

"Uh-huh." He brushed a curl out of my face, his touch as delicate as a gentle breeze. "You're actually kind of pretty when you're flustered. Your eyes flash. Your cheeks fill with color. Your lips…" His voice trailed off as he propped his arm up just above my head and stared at that particular piece of my anatomy.

My tongue darted out to lick them before I could catch myself. "Are you going to kiss me again?"

Everything about him said yes, from the hunger in his eyes to the way he leaned closer to me. "Do you want me to?"

Yes, yes, yes, yes! My crazed hormones screamed, but my mouth refused to work.

Brett must have taken my silence for consent because he continued to close the gap until his lips grazed mine. The kiss bore the same uncertainty, the same restraint as before. He pulled back, waiting to see how I would react.

I pressed my arms against my sides to keep from jumping him like I did last time.

However, when I didn't knee him in the groin, he repeated the kiss. This time, he was out to make a bold statement. No hesitancy. No restraint. Just his lips firmly molding mine, teasing me, tempting me.

The pit of my stomach throbbed as he continued to kiss me, slow and steady in contrast with the disjointed fluttering of my heart. We both managed to keep our hands off of each other—mine at my sides and his above my head. Perhaps it was our way of making sure our shirts stayed on this time while still thoroughly enjoying the connection.

Brett ended the contact between our lips, but he didn't retreat. His face hovered near mine, the tips of our noses touching. "You drive me nuts, Alexis Wyndham."

"Glad to know I'm not the only one who feels that way."

He was moving forward to kiss me again when his mom called his name from the end of the hallway. He bolted from me like I'd burned him, a curse dropping from those delectable lips of his.

I slid down the wall onto the mattress and managed to hug the doll to my chest just as his mom opened the door.

She glanced at me, then at him, and back again. "Brett, you know the rules about having guests over past eight o'clock on a school night."

"Yes, Mum, but Alexis is here helping me with our class assignment that's due tomorrow."

I did a double take at the screen. Somehow, he'd managed to hide all the open windows pertaining to the voyeur and pull up the worksheet on stress relief that we were supposed to be working on.

She scanned the homework, then looked back at me as though she was trying to spot any evidence of unscholarly activities.

I forced a smile on my face and hugged the doll even tighter. "We're just about to wrap things up, Mrs. Pederson."

She gave Brett a stern glance, wagging her finger at him. "Fifteen more minutes, and then she has to go. You need to rest for the game tomorrow."

When she left, she didn't close the door all the way.

I was glad she didn't. It would be too tempting to pick up where we left off if she had.

Brett lowered the window with the assignment and brought back Adam Kozlovsky's ID. "Back to this—I did a little more digging on him, and I wanted to intercede on his behalf."

"Wait a minute." I jumped to my feet and whirled his chair around. "Just a few minutes ago, you said you'd want revenge if it were your sisters. Why is my mine any different? I mean, besides the fact Taylor's a hot mess and Sarah seems to have her shit together?"

"I'm not going to go into details," he said slowly, the wariness behind his words hinting at how much those details had him on edge, "but I really think you should handle him delicately."

"Give me a damn good reason why I shouldn't plaster his face all over the front page of my blog."

Brett leaned back in his chair and rubbed his eyes as though trying to reason with me was the most exhausting thing he'd ever done. Maybe it was. I was notoriously stubborn. But in this case, I had the upper hand. I had justice on my side. "Remember what I told you last week about compassion and happiness?"

"Are you suggesting I show this guy compassion after what he did?"

He leveled his gaze with mine, dead serious for once. "Yes."

"Why?" We stared each other down for several breaths, and when he couldn't give me a good reason, I turned for the door. "I have to go and re-write my editorial into an exposé and get it up before midnight."

A hand clamped around my wrist before I made it to the hallway. Brett pulled me back and blocked my escape. "For someone who gets her kicks picking on the in-crowd, I'd expected better from you, but I guess I was wrong."

"Excuse me?" I tried to get around him, but he was bigger than me and took up the entire doorway.

"You heard me, Lexi. You're one of the few people in school who has power—true power—to shape the school. You could be the hero for every unpopular kid in school, but you're too narrow-minded to see that."

"And what about you? You're the most popular guy in school. Perhaps you should be taking some of your own advice."

"That's what I'm trying to do." He waited until I gave up trying to get past him before continuing. "I know who Adam is because he's frequently a target of some of my teammates."

"And you condone this bullying?"

"No—not at all. I try to stop it as much as I can, but I can't be everywhere at once." He licked his lips, his face paling. "But when I did some digging in his school records, I found out some information I shouldn't have seen."

"Like what?"

"I've already gone out on a limb for you, and I'm not going to reveal any more damaging evidence." He raked his fingers through his hair, but it did little to hide the tremor in his hand. "But let's just say he's pretty fucked up. And if you publicly humiliate him like you're planning on doing, it may just tip him over the edge."

Even though he was doing his best to protect the kid, he'd told me enough to chill my blood. My anger congealed into a lump of fear centered in the middle of my throat. I had to swallow hard to choke it back down and find my voice again. "He can't get away with what he's done."

"I'm not suggesting you let him, nor am I condoning his actions. I'm just asking you to consider the consequences of your actions and give compassion a try over ball-busting for once."

Talk about ruining my perfect plans for revenge. I'd been so dead set on making that asshole pay, but somehow, Brett had me hesitating, thinking about the consequences of my actions. If I stayed here any longer, he'd probably talk me into treating Adam Kozlovsky to fro-yo and talking about our feelings. "I have to go before your mom comes back."

This time, he didn't stop me.

I went home and fired up my laptop, rewriting my editorial into a piece that would condemn Adam Kozlovsky. As I tried to paint a picture of the misogynistic voyeur I pictured him to be, I pulled out last year's yearbook and tried to find more information on him. I found him listed as a member of the chess club and the computer club, but when I looked at the pictures, he was absent. Last year's photo looked the same as this year's. Same frumpy appearance. Same blank, disengaged expression.

I stared at his photo, wondering the reason behind it. Brett mentioned he'd been bullied, but so had other kids in the school, especially freshmen. That didn't necessarily translate into fucked up.

Consider the consequences of my actions, huh?

I went back to my blog post. If I hit send now, everyone in the school would know what he'd done. Girls would never give him the time of day after this, and since the main target of his videos was the cheerleading squad, I'm sure some of their boyfriends would place him at the top of their shit list.

He probably wouldn't be able to walk down the hallways without getting harassed by someone.

Repressed memories followed me from junior high when the in-crowd had chosen me as their target for harassment. That sick feeling I had in my stomach every time I walked through the door hit me again. I doubled over, my eyes wincing hard enough to squeeze out tears. I'd hated my life then. Thankfully, I'd had family to support me, to help me overcome that. I'd been strong enough to rise above the bullying.

The nausea gradually faded as I pushed back those memories and focused on how far I'd come.

I glanced back at the photo. Was he strong enough to do that? Or would I only make things worse? Would I push him over the edge like Brett had warned?

The clock read 11:45 p.m. I posted a quick note on my blog that my usual Friday post would be late and went to work rewriting my story.

> *Last week, I deviated from the norm here at the Eastline Spy and unintentionally became a conspirator in scandal. But now it's time to come clean. It's time to reveal some uncomfortable truths. And it's time to make people realize that certain things cross the line of what's acceptable.*

My fingers trembled as I typed. I read through it one more time, satisfied with what I managed to come up with, and scheduled the blog post to go live at the start of fourth period.

"How about some hot and heavy action in the principal's office? Check out the before and after pictures of Mr. Collins and Mrs. Goodell. Either they were experimenting with some hair gel, or something else must have disheveled their immaculate coifs. Of course, she might just be grabbing his tie like a leash as an odd way of straightening it, too."

The Eastline Spy
May, Junior Year

Chapter 18

I woke up the next morning with an odd feeling of peace, especially considering how little sleep I'd gotten between my blog post and the doll. I got dressed, strapped the baby carrier to my chest for the last time, and drove to school. I waited for that odd flop in my stomach, that sense of second-guessing my decision, but it didn't come. After agonizing for hours on what to do with Adam Kozlovsky, I knew I'd made the right decision.

There was no need for a handoff that morning, so I was surprised to find Brett waiting for me at my locker, wearing his game day jersey. "Alexis, please—"

"I already scheduled my post, Brett." I opened my locker and switched out my books for the morning. "There's nothing you can do now to change that."

A look of defeat crossed his features. He looked down at the ground. "And what did you decide to do?"

I slammed my locker closed. I could tell him, but I decided it would be more fun to let him stew about it, especially since he enjoyed flustering me so much last night. "You'll find out when the blog post goes live at lunch."

As I walked off, he called after me, "Don't forget to do your part of the assignment."

I stopped dead in my tracks. I'd been so focused on nailing the person behind the videos, I'd forgotten all about that.

I slid into my desk for first period and fired up my laptop. Somehow, scrambling to finish an assignment at the last minute wasn't my idea of stress reduction. I started listing things that sounded good at relieving stress. A massage. A walk in the park. A funny movie. All very generic and bland.

Then I peeked over at Brett's list, and something inside me shifted gears. His was very personal, very specific.

Throwing the perfect spiral pass.

Playing games with my sisters.

Finding the perfect chocolate chip to frozen yogurt ratio.

Watching the entire Lord of the Rings *trilogy in one sitting.*

Getting a new high score on my favorite video game.

Kissing a pretty girl.

Making someone smile.

Spending time with someone who truly gets me.

I choked up a little as I came to the final item on his list. It reminded me of what he'd said Monday afternoon before leaving my house, that I was one of the few people he could be himself around.

How many people in Eastline could say they knew the real Brett? The Brett who played with his sisters? The Brett who wasn't always so sure what the future held? The Brett who wanted to be more than just a football star? The Brett who was closet geek and hacker extraordinaire?

I reread the last item on his list and realized I felt the same. As much as he left me flustered and frustrated, Brett sometimes understood me better than Morgan and Richard. And if Monday was any indication, I was actually going to miss spending time with him once we wrapped up this project.

I went back to my list and changed it around, making it as specific as Brett's. And when I got to the end, I added, *Doing something nice for someone else.*

***

Brett slid quietly into the seat next to me just as the bell rang for fourth period. "Glad to be done with this?"

"The doll, yes."

An amused glint filled his eyes. "Just the doll?"

"For now."

He looked away. "Listen, about last night—"

"There's nothing more to talk about, Brett. You made your case."

"But I wasn't finished."

My heart jumped, stopping the air from entering my lungs. Was he going to harp on me more about exposing the voyeur? Or was he going to bring up the kiss?

Thankfully, the intercom at the front of the class crackled to life and interrupted Mr. DePaul. "Will Alexis Wyndham please report to Principal Lee's office?"

My heart skipped another beat, and this time, it had nothing to do with Brett. I'd never been called to the principal's office. I gathered my things, leaving the doll behind with Brett, and made my way to the door with everyone in the class watching me like I was a criminal on death row on my way to the chair.

Of course, when they call you to the principal's office, they don't bring you in right away. They let you stew outside for a good thirty minutes, watching his secretary answer the phone and type away on her computer, perhaps hoping the anxiety of being there will make you more compliant to his will.

Or make you less hostile.

Unfortunately, it had the opposite effect on me. I'd done nothing wrong. By the time the door opened, I was ready to test out my Queen B powers on Principal Lee and see if he responded the way the rest of the students did.

He wasn't easily intimidated by my "eat shit and die" glare. Instead, he kept his face unreadable as he pointed to the chair across from his desk. "Have a seat, Ms. Wyndham."

"Listen, I don't know why you've called me here, but it's interfering with my academic achievement, and I don't appreciate you keeping me from the stimulating discussions in health class." I sat down, crossed my legs, and waited for him to respond to my opening argument.

He merely narrowed his eyes and seemed to take even longer to return to his chair. "Will you please check your attitude at the door?"

"I'm here to learn, Mr. Lee, not twiddle my thumbs outside your office."

"I could suspend you."

"For what? Being a voracious student?" I smiled sweetly, daring him to. I could use a vacation from this place. But just to cover my bases, I reached into my pocket and hit the record button on my phone. If I was going to take the heat for this, I wanted everything documented.

"No, for this." He tapped his computer screen that displayed my blog post. "If word gets out about this to the local media—"

"Are you suggesting I don't report the truth?"

"I'm suggesting you keep your stories to subjects that do not slander our school."

I pulled out my notepad and started scribbling notes. If he wanted to play hardball, I'd give him something to sweat about. "So you're saying I should censor my blog?"

"No, I'm not saying that."

"But you are restricting my First Amendment rights to free speech." I scribbled some more notes. I already knew what next week's blog post would be about.

"Put your pen down, Ms. Wyndham, and answer my questions." His voice darkened. He was playing bad cop, and there wasn't a good cop in sight to rescue me.

I set the notepad in my lap. "Ask away, Mr. Lee."

"How long have you known about those videos?"

"They first came to my attention last week. One of the victims was quite traumatized to discover them."

"And why didn't you bring it to my attention then?"

"Because I wanted to handle it." I shifted in my seat and re-crossed my legs.

A bead of sweat rolled down his temple. "No, because you wanted to make me look like an idiot, just like you did my predecessor."

"No offense, Mr. Lee, but you do a good job of doing that on your own if you have no idea what's being posted about your school on YouTube."

I was pushing his buttons, and I enjoyed it. It seemed my Queen B powers weren't limited to just the student body. And based on the way the conversation was heading, I knew what he'd eventually ask. However, I was still trying to decide how much information to give him when the moment came.

He blotted his forehead with a tissue. "I want you to

remove this post."

I picked up my notepad again. "And we're back to censoring the presses."

"No, I'm trying to protect the reputation of this school."

"Correction—you're trying to protect your reputation as principal of this school."

He pointed a shaking finger at the screen, his face paling with each word. "If there is any truth to your allegations—"

"And there is."

"—I'm going to have to answer to the school board about this."

"Probably not a bad idea, especially considering how easy it was for the person to use the school's network to record and upload videos from the girls' locker room." I decided to play up the moment, steering the conversation away from Principal Lee's wounded pride and toward a solution. "As a female student of Eastline High, I have never felt more violated in all my life, and I wasn't even one of the women featured in the videos."

"So you mentioned in your article. But you managed to leave out some important details."

"Such as?"

"Where are the videos now?"

"I had someone remove them for the sake of the victims."

That seemed to ease Principal Lee's fear. He leaned back in his chair. "And how did you manage that?"

"Please, Mr. Lee—this is the land of computer geeks galore. It wasn't that hard to find someone to do that."

"I need a name." He watched me with glittering eyes, trying to ruffle my feathers with silent intimidation.

He obviously didn't know who he was up against. "Would Batman work for you?"

His expression darkened. "That's not what I was talking about, Ms. Wyndham."

"You just said you needed a name."

"This is not like you. I've read your posts in the past, and you've always been eager to name names and point fingers. What are you trying to hide?"

"This is different."

"No, this is a major issue I'm going to have to answer for, and I'm not letting you leave until you give me the information I need to resolve it. Who helped you track down the person behind the videos?"

I gulped. Brett would be in some serious trouble if I named him. Suspension would surely ruin his chances for a scholarship, not to mention his reputation if people learned what a geek he really was. "I'm not going to reveal my sources."

"Then tell me who's behind the videos."

I remembered Brett's warning about pushing Adam past the tipping point. "If I tell you, will you promise to handle the matter discreetly?"

"Ms. Wyndham, you destroyed any hope for discretion when you published that article."

"Actually, no, I didn't. I exposed a problem, and I discovered the person behind it. He's a minor, though, and under the law, he's allowed certain protections, which is why I didn't reveal his name. Not to mention, there's a high probability things could get worse if people found out he was behind the videos."

"I'll be the judge of that." He nodded to the screen. "If you refuse to give me a name, then I'll have to assume you're an accomplice to the matter and punish you accordingly."

"And I go to the media and let them know about the cover-up at Eastline."

"If anyone's covering anything up, it's you."

"I'm willing to give you his name, but only if you promise not to draw any unnecessary attention to him."

Principal Lee's brows moved in opposite directions—one up and one down. "I'm having a hard time figuring out your motives."

"Well, if you'd just asked nicely, I would have explained them to you."

"Why do I find that hard to believe?" He crossed his arms. "Explain them, then."

"The reason I tried to handle this myself is because my sister was one of the victims, and I wanted to spare her any further embarrassment. I'd thought I had taken care of it last week, but it became clear earlier this week that the person behind the videos couldn't take a hint. So, I launched my investigation, and thanks to the wonder of IP addresses, my accomplice was able to track him down."

Principal Lee nodded. "Go on."

"But when my accomplice realized who the person was, he was only willing to give me a name after I promised to handle the matter delicately. So now, I'm asking the same of you."

"You're going to talk in circles until I agree, aren't you?"

"You're the one who wants a name, and I want to prevent any more drama in the hallways."

He swiveled back and forth in his chair, his arms still crossed, and stared at the headline I'd created about our X-rated Peeping Tom. "Ms. Wyndham, what are you planning on doing with your life?"

"I haven't the faintest idea." I remembered what Brett had said about me being a ball-buster and caught myself grinning. "Maybe I'll become Attorney General one day."

"Well, if you're serious about the legal field, you need to be prepared to name sources if you wish to be credible."

The tension eased from my shoulders. I'd worn him down, even though he wasn't ready to admit it just yet. "I understand that."

"If I agree to handle the student behind this appropriately, will you give me his name?"

I nodded and took a deep breath. "Adam Kozlovsky."

He jumped as though I'd zapped him with a Taser. I had no idea what was in those confidential files Brett had stumbled upon, but it was quite clear Principal Lee did. And based on the way the color seemed to drain from the principal's face, it wasn't pretty. "Thank you, Ms. Wyndham. I'll speak to him about this matter right away."

I pointed to my blog on his screen. "And no censoring of the press?"

He shook his head. "But I ask you not to speak to the news media about this if word gets out. Let me handle it."

"Of course." I pulled my phone out of my pocket and stopped the recording. "It was a pleasure talking with you, Principal Lee, but I need to go back to my academic studies now." And back to my last day working with Brett.

The bell rang, indicating the end of fourth period, and I fought back the sigh of resignation. My class project time with Brett was now officially over. It was time to resume my role as the Queen B.

I just hoped he'd notice what I'd done.

"Raise your hand if you're a female student who's ever gotten the heebie-jeebies in Mr. Rodchenko's class from the way he's always staring your chest. Eyes up here, please."

The Eastline Spy
January, Freshman Year

Chapter 19

Brett was leaning on the wall outside the office when I finally re-emerged, his attention focused on the screen of his tablet.

It was lunch, and students funneled through the hallways toward their favorite dining location. They huddled in groups, some of them with tablets or phones in their hands, their shocked whispers buzzing like a swarm of flies. What shocked me, though, was the fact Brett was without his usual entourage. No Summer draping all over him. No teammates laughing and high-fiving. Just him, standing alone.

I approached him. "Looking for me?"

He raised his eyes from the screen and turned it off. "Yeah, actually, I was. Can we go someplace private to talk?

I was exhausted, and I knew if I took him back to my place, I wouldn't be able to say no to my hormones if he tried to kiss me again. And if he was willing to be seen waiting outside the principal's office for me, maybe I would be willing to be seen in public with him. "We can do a lap around the football field, if you want."

"You do realize that people will see us—together—outside of class?"

"Yeah, I think I can risk it this one time."

Something faded from his eyes. He actually looked disappointed when I didn't suggest we go back to my house. But as quickly as it appeared, it was gone. "Sure."

We crossed the campus to the stadium. Groups of students hung out on the bleachers, enjoying the mid-September sunshine while they could. Brett and I drew their attention as we approached, but no one bothered us. I expected to feel awkward or paranoid from all the eyes on us, but walking with Brett felt comfortable, natural.

Right, like we belonged together.

Yeah, I'd fallen for him.

Hard.

But I was still too proud to admit it. Just call me Mr. Darcy.

We were halfway around the field before I finally asked, "So, what did you want to talk about?"

"You didn't name him," he said quietly, staring at the ground.

"No, I didn't."

"Why?"

I gave him a wry smile. "Maybe I decided to give this compassion thing a try, see if it makes me happier."

He looked up, mirroring my expression. "I'm glad you did."

"I can't go making a habit of it, though. I mean, if word gets out that I was actually, you know, *nice*, no one would respect me anymore."

"Heaven forbid," he teased.

"Besides, I only did it out of self-preservation. I didn't want that kid going postal on us or doing anything drastic."

"What you're trying to say is that you did the right thing to protect him."

"And believe me, it was harder than I thought it would be, especially with Principal Lee threatening me with suspension for my article."

A line formed between Brett's brows. "Was that why he wanted to see you?"

"Yeah, he wanted names."

He drew to a stop, the corners of his mouth tilting down. "And what did you tell him?"

"Don't worry, Superman, this Lois Lane didn't reveal your secret identity. I made him promise to treat Adam with care and not blow things out of proportion. As soon as I gave him the name, he seemed to understand where I was coming from."

Brett nodded once, swallowing hard in the process and making me wonder again what he'd accidentally read. He resumed walking. "So you did this purely to save yourself?"

I rocked back and forth on my feet, creating an opportunity to bump into him. "Well, maybe I did it as a favor to you, too."

"You did a favor for me?"

"You asked me so nicely last night."

He chuckled and went back to looking at the ground, his thumbs running up and down the straps of his backpack. "You know, I wasn't asked to switch names with you. I'm the one who asked to switch."

I ambled along a few steps, trying to swallow past the jumble of emotions that suddenly clogged my throat. "Why?"

"Because I wanted to get to know you better. And I'm glad I did. You're actually kind of cool."

"You're just now realizing that?"

My quip helped break some of the tension, and we stopped at the far corner of the field near the scoreboard. It offered us some protection from prying eyes, which I welcomed.

Brett turned to face me. "You're not going to make this easy for me, are you?"

I set my messenger bag down on the grass. Something told me we were going to be here for a while. "I never make anything easy for anybody."

"No shit." He kicked at the ground. "I know you don't want to talk about it, but there's a definite chemistry between us."

My stomach knotted. "You mean what happened in the janitor's closet?"

"And my bedroom."

"And I bet you were hoping we could continue to hook up?"

"Yes—I mean, no—" He slung his backpack on the ground again and moved toward me.

My head swam, and warning bells went off. I backed away before he kissed me in front of everyone in the school. It was one thing to suffer temporary insanity behind closed doors. It was an entirely different thing to lose it on campus where other students could see us, even if the scoreboard was partially concealing us. "Stop, Brett, please."

My voice sounded high, strained, panicked.

But it had the desired effect. He froze right where he was. Then his face hardened. "Damn it, Lexi, what is your problem?"

"This is my problem." I pointed to the buildings of the school, sweeping my finger across the campus at all the students. "If someone saw us kissing, do you realize what a field day they'd have with it?"

"So?"

"Well, then forget the student body in general. What would Summer do? Sanchez? The rest of the team? Do you realize how much shit they'd give you for being with me?"

"I can handle them." He took another step toward me, but I retreated. "Scared?"

"No, but I don't need the extra headache."

"Bullshit." He crossed his arms, growing more distant.

And as much as my heart ached to witness the change in him, my mind rejoiced. I'd keep pushing him away. It was best for both of us.

"Why are you afraid to admit you have a thing for me?" he asked.

I wanted to lie and say I didn't, but there was too much evidence against me. He'd seen how I responded to his touch, to his kiss. He knew the difference between my furious face and my flustered face, and he knew how easily I melted into his arms.

I leaned back against the scoreboard and sighed. "Fine, I admit I have a thing for you. I'll go as far as to admit that I really like kissing you."

"Then why are you acting this way?"

"Because when we're together, it's too intense, too hot. It's like throwing a lighted match into a warehouse full of fireworks—one big, beautiful explosion that will leave nothing but ashes once the smoke clears." I paused then added, "And I don't want to do that to you."

"Who says it has to end that way?" He tilted my chin up until my eyes locked with his. "I'm willing to chance it if you are."

"Do you realize what you're saying?"

He nodded, his expression soft yet serious. "I really like you, Lexi. You've always intrigued me. That's why I offered to switch names with the person who drew yours. I wanted to get to know you, to spend time with you."

I turned away before I crumbled under his sweet words, before he saw the tears gathering in my eyes. "I'm not ready to take that step, Brett."

His hands fell to his side, and the ache returned to my chest. I doubted any other girl in school would've turned Brett down, but that wasn't who I was. I was hard. I was cruel. I didn't let people get to me. I was the Queen B.

And at the moment, I hated being that.

So much, that I took his hand in mine before he drifted too far away. "I'm sorry, Brett, but I need time to get my head around all this."

He didn't have to say he thought I was a coward. I saw it in his eyes.

I tightened my grip on his hand. "Please?"

"So what are you suggesting?"

"That we start by being friends."

One dark brow rose. "Friends?"

I nodded.

"You know that's the nice way of softening a brush-off, Lexi."

The corners of my mouth twitched. "Maybe for other girls, but I'm not like them."

"You're not kidding," he said with a grin. "But I'm willing to try it."

The warmth returned between us, his fingers squeezing mine. "You know, it's quite an honor to be one of my friends. You've joined an elite group."

"Just promise me I won't have to watch any of Richard's cheerleading routines."

I laughed and then looked down to where our fingers were still entwined. My breath hitched. I forced myself to untangle my hand from his. "We should start moving before the gossip mill starts spinning."

"Yeah, I suppose you're right." He picked up my bag and handed it to me as we resumed our course around the field. "Although I meant what I said—I'm willing to chance it if you are."

"I'll keep that in mind the next time my hormones get the better of me and demand a hookup."

"Drag me into the janitor's closet anytime you want, Lexi. Maybe then I can convince you how good we could be together."

"You are so full of yourself." But deep inside, I hoped he would. My lips already tingled at the thought of another make out session.

"So, are you going to come to the game tonight?"

"Keep dreaming."

"Not even to cheer for one of your friends?"

I grinned. "Nope."

We'd barely reached the edge of the field before Summer and her entourage (which included my sister) surrounded us. She looped her arm through Brett's, letting her minions push me to the edge of the crowd. "There you are, Brett. I'd heard that you were stuck out here with *her*, and I came to rescue you."

"Scared I'll steal him away?" I countered, sharing a secret grin with Brett.

"Someone like you doesn't stand a chance." She whirled so her skirt flared around her hips, showing off her bronzed legs. "Come along, Brett. You don't have to hang around her anymore now that your stupid baby project's done."

A dozen comebacks sat poised on my tongue, most of them revolving around Summer's silicone parts. They stayed in the recesses of my mind, ready for another day. I already knew I had the upper hand. Let her live in her delusions a bit longer.

Brett offered a wave from the center of the cheerleading squad. "See you around, Lexi."

I saluted him and strolled off in the opposite direction. I was Queen B, after all. I wasn't about to give that title up.

But I was willing to try something new, including being friends with a guy I used to think was the epitome of everything I was against. Turns out I might have been wrong about him. And since this was my final year of the level of hell Dante missed, I might as well have a good time dancing in the flames.

As soon as I got to my car, I pulled out my phone and dialed one of the few numbers I had on speed dial. "Hey, Richard, do you need a ride to the football game tonight?"

I wasn't finished with Brett Pederson.

A Note to Readers

Dear Reader,

Thank you so much for reading *Confessions of a Queen B**. I hope you enjoyed it and look forward to reading the next book in the series, *The Queen B* Strikes Back*. If you did, please leave a review at the store where you bought this book or on Goodreads.

I love to hear from readers. You can find me on Facebook and Twitter, or you can email me using the contact form on my website, www.CristaMcHugh.com.

If you would like to be the first to know about new releases or be entered into exclusive contests, please sign up for my newsletter using the contact form on my website at http.//bit.ly/19EJAW8.

--Crista

Don't miss the next book in the Queen B* series…

The Queen B*

Strikes Back

The Queen B*, Book 2

Alexis Wyndham isn't quite sure what to think about her "friendship" with star quarterback, Brett Pederson. Sure, he has more brains than the entire football team combined. Not to mention the fact he's a great kisser. When he asks her to help him with his college admission essays, she isn't sure if he's doing it to spend more time with her or if he's just using her for her intelligence. But after her nemesis, Summer Hoyt, makes it clear she's not finished chasing after Brett, the war is on, and the head cheerleader will find out that hell hath no fury like a Queen B*tch.

Coming in September 2015…

Sign up for Crista's Newsletter to be the first to know when *The Queen B* Strikes Back* is available.

Author Bio

Growing up in small town Alabama, Crista relied on storytelling as a natural way for her to pass the time and keep her two younger sisters entertained.

She currently lives in the Audi-filled suburbs of Seattle with her husband and two children, maintaining her alter ego of mild-mannered physician by day while she continues to pursue writing on nights and weekends.

Just for laughs, here are some of the jobs she's had in the past to pay the bills: barista, bartender, sommelier, stagehand, actress, morgue attendant, and autopsy assistant.

And she's also a recovering LARPer. (She blames it on her crazy college days)

For the latest updates, deleted scenes, and answers to any burning questions you have, please check out her webpage, www.CristaMcHugh.com.

Sign up for Crista's 99c New Release Newsletter at http://bit.ly/19EJAW8

Find Crista online at:

Twitter: twitter.com/crista_mchugh

Facebook: www.facebook.com/CristaMcHugh

CPSIA information can be obtained
at www.ICGtesting.com
Printed in the USA
FSOW02n0500040615
7640FS